William Ivers is a teacher and award-winning playwright. He lives in Hooksett, NH, with his wife and children.

To Maria

William Ivers

PIERCED GIRLS

AUSTIN MACAULEY PUBLISHERS™

LONDON * CAMBRIDGE * NEW YORK * SHARJAH

Ordering Information
Quantity sales: Special discounts are available on quantity purchases by corporations, associations, and others. For details, contact the publisher at the address below.

Publisher's Cataloging-in-Publication data
Ivers, William
Pierced Girls

ISBN 9798889104025 (Paperback)
ISBN 9798889104032 (ePub e-book)

Library of Congress Control Number: 2023919127

www.austinmacauley.com/us

First Published 2024
Austin Macauley Publishers LLC
40 Wall Street, 33rd Floor, Suite 3302
New York, NY 10005
USA

mail-usa@austinmacauley.com
+1 (646) 5125767

Walter Freeman
Heidi Grant
John Sefel
Brandi DiPrete

Chapter One

The concert band was warming up as I stood under the bleachers, slouched in my cap and gown, wondering why I was even there. High-school graduations, like dance recitals, princess birthday parties, and so many other so-called special occasions, were for the other girls in that line—girls with gym memberships, cute puppies, and prom dates. These girls tanned on school vacations and lived on streets with cul-de-sacs in nice houses with moms who weren't in and out of prison or rehab and with dads who weren't dead.

Graduation ceremonies, like so many *normie* things in life, weren't for girls from the children's home. Girls like me.

Then why torture myself? Was I really buying into all that *Oh, the Places You'll Go!* kind of crap, thinking a diploma with my name on it meant something? Maybe I thought it would make me feel normal for a little while. But normal was never my thing. I was a walking anachronism, a punk rock girl beamed up from 1979 with green hair, a spiked leather jacket, with weird obsessions with old literature and black and white films, topped off with a sneer that told the world to stay back.

I was bad at normal. So when the band started *Pomp and Circumstance*, as I took my place in line with all those normal kids, the whole thing felt like a farce. Nothing was about to change for this girl. My life was still a bad song on repeat. Anxious as hell, I snuck another Xanax, hoping it would trigger the two already in my system. Then, out of nowhere, I heard, "Hey, Sheena!"

Convinced I was busted, I turned around and saw Bryce Whittaker, a guy I hooked up with at a house party during my junior year. We never talked after that, mostly because he ditched me once I dozed. I found myself the next morning hanging off a dirty living room couch surrounded by hungover kids I didn't know. What he had to say to me now, a year later, I had no idea.

He gave me that dumb nod-up thing that guys do.

I pretended I didn't know his name. "It's Bryce, right?"

"How've you been?" I hated to admit it, but he was still sort of cute with those glassy blue eyes and his long brown hair. But the man-bun was tragic.

"Just wonderful," I said with just a hint of sarcasm.

After bobbing our heads awkwardly at each other, he said, "Do you believe all this?"

"Believe all what?" I didn't want him to think we were on the same page.

"Graduating, college, life. What we've been through. It's so crazy and a little scary, huh?" He spoke like we were old friends.

"Sure, whatever, I guess." I didn't know how to react to such blatant high school phoniness. I barely knew the guy and out of nowhere, he's talking like we'd been through a war together. What happened on that boozy night— encouraged by whatever was in those red Solo cups—just sort of happened. It was a little random. A little nothing. It didn't mean anything to me. Or so I told myself.

He paused and said, "Next chapters, am I right? New horizons." It was like he was dictating a Hallmark card.

"Oh, the places we'll go!" Strange he wasn't picking up on my sarcasm, which was thicker now.

Still, the conversation wasn't over. He started to get personal. "What are you gonna do next?"

"Not sure. Maybe get a bagel."

He laughed. "You know what I mean! Like *next* next."

I shrugged. "Oh, *next*! You mean like with all my big dreams? Haven't really thought about it. Just trying to get through today." This was a total lie. 'Next' was all I ever thought about, and how no one was waiting in line to pay my college tuition and how my dreams of becoming a music teacher were already dead in the water, and how I blew my chance at any scholarship money. I suppose loans were a possibility, but did I really want to bury myself deeper?

Now this Bryce guy, hell-bent on making this an actual conversation, started talking about *his* college plans. "It's state school for me, but what can you do?" He said this like it was a horrible thing, like he was getting drafted.

"Yeah, well, break a leg," I said, thinking it was the perfect note to end on.

But, to my absolute horror, he went *there*. "So, about what happened, you know, at that party. I never forgot that night. No lie."

My mouth fell open. I wanted to take his gold cord and strangle him. Why was he bringing that up? Was he going to say *We'll always have Paris* next?

Did he think I was heartbroken or even cared? Our little session meant as little to me as I'm sure it did to him. *Less* than zero.

"Don't worry about it," I said. "Seriously, don't."

"I should've called or texted or something."

"No, really, *don't* worry about it."

"You kinda deserved a text at least."

"Kinda?"

"You did. And I feel shitty about not sending one."

"Oh, that text would've meant the world to me," I said with as much vicious, obvious sarcasm I could generate, which was a lot.

Picking up on it this time, he was very weirded out and said, "Don't be like that. I just—"

"Felt bad for me?"

"No, not like that. I just didn't want you to feel—"

"Used? Ditched?" I said, interrupting him. "Think that's new to me?"

I immediately felt lame for being so dramatic. I also felt a little guilty because I think it made him feel like shit, but it did make him finally walk away. Whatever. It wasn't like I'd see him again. Like I said, the whole thing was really nothing.

As the band played its dirge, some teacher sent us marching through the bleachers and onto the field as moms, dads, and grandparents all watched, many of them smiling behind camera phones. It felt like I was crashing a party, a costume party with everyone dressed in gold cords, scholarship pins, and caps decorated with glitter and paint. The night before I considered gluing the Dead Kennedys logo to mine but decided there wasn't anything less punk.

The ceremony dragged on with each speaker—the principal, class president, and the valedictorian—carrying on like it was a cliché contest. But I guess that's exactly what the whole thing was—a cliché. And maybe I was a cliché, too. I was that silent girl. Every class had one: the weird girl in the corner who falls through the cracks and gets pissed off at the world, the one who pops into your head ten years later and you think, *I wonder what ever happened to that weird girl—what was her name? Sheena?*

Sitting there, I found more reasons to be resentful and pissed off. I was pissed that no one was pointing an iPhone at me, pissed I had no money for college, pissed that everything seemed rigged.

So it was bad timing when our class president, Hannah Ackerman, squealed, "Congratulations, class of 2018!" urging the graduates to toss their caps into the air while I just sat there like an idiot with all my negative thoughts ruminating. It was seriously a bad time for the chick behind me to rip off my cap and chuck it ten rows backward like she was doing me a favor. Her timing was so bad in fact that, without hesitation, I stood up and slapped the side of her head, sending her tumbling over two folding chairs and flat onto the grass.

The band and the cheering made it so only about twelve kids noticed, but as those twelve stared at me like I was a psycho, I decided to split, to slip through the crowd unnoticed by my teachers and peers—one last time.

I sprinted back under the bleachers and through the crowded parking lot, running in between the parked cars like it was a prison break. If anyone noticed a crazed teen girl ripping off her graduation gown like it had the plague, casting it onto a minivan, tears flying off her face, no one did a thing about it. I jumped into my junky old Honda Civic and drove away, making it official. I was done with high school, forever. Or maybe high school was done with me.

Chapter Two

My father was legendary punk rocker, Joey Ramone—at least this is what my mother told me. Sure, mom wasn't the most reliable source, considering she spent most of my childhood strung out on heroin, but I still believed her. And why the hell not? You can't be wrong about everything, and situationally, it all checks out. Mom was living in NYC at the time, playing bass for a quasi-successful punk band called Slug Sex.

One night, after opening for the Ramones, she became one of the countless women to pogo in bed with dad, Mr. Punk rock himself, who probably never even bothered to learn her name. Mom said this all went down in October of 2000, so the fact my birthday was nine months later on 15 June was all the proof I needed. Cancer took my dad away in April of 2001, two months before I was dropped into this sideshow.

From all the YouTube interviews I've seen, dad seemed like my kind of guy—chill, funny, and somewhat fragile behind that punk persona. Knowing him would have been cool but his music was always there for me. When things were really shitty, if I felt off-the-charts-scared or alone, I would talk to him, and he would talk back and say the things I'd imagine he'd say. Or the things I was too afraid to say myself. So what if it was all in my head? It felt real, especially once the Xanax kicked in.

So as I drove away from the graduation ceremony, a voice from the passenger seat startled me. The Xanax had finally kicked in.

You left your diploma at the school, kiddo.

It was dad. He was a sight for sore eyes with his long raven hair that flowed onto his black leather jacket. His long legs in tight, ripped jeans were cramped up against the dashboard. His eyes were always hidden behind dark shades, but I imagined they were kind, deep eyes. Eyes that saw through all the bullshit. Eyes that only saw the best version of me.

"Whatever," I said. "It's not like I have a wall to hang it up on. Not anymore." Now that I was eighteen, I'd soon be out of the foster system for good and would have to give up my bed at the children's home. But I didn't care. Part of me was ready to move on from all that. I was sick of sharing spaces with kids I didn't know and following rules made up to keep girls like me out of trouble. It was definitely time for a scene change.

A piece of paper can't define you anyway, he said.

"Tell that to the college admissions boards," I said, holding up a brochure that was stuffed into the cup holder.

What do they know? he said. *Who needs them?*

"I do."

Nah, just another one of society's little games.

"Yeah, yeah, I know, Dad. I've heard this before." I stuffed the brochure into my coat pocket. "It might be time to get real. I can't even get through my own high school graduation like a normal person. It's like I have a talent for conflict."

He laughed. *You say that like it's a bad thing,* he said. *That chick landing on her ass was the best part of the ceremony!*

"I do these crazy things and feel instantly guilty."

It's all in your head, he smirked. He was always smirking. *Don't feel guilty. The system is rigged against scrubs like us,* he said.

"System?"

Dad was banging on his knees like they were bongos. Nothing seemed to get to him.

That's right, kid. The system, the machine. It's all bullshit.

"So what do I do about it?"

You laugh at it, write a song about it, and you fight it, he said while searching for something worth listening to on my car radio. *Don't they play rock and roll anymore?*

"Fighting is getting me nowhere, Dad," I said.

He stopped on a station that was playing *Catch a Wave* by The Beach Boys, looking very pleased with himself. *You're doing okay, Sheena,* he said. *Keep doing your thing.*

"Whatever my thing is, it's not working."

Sure it is, he protested. He turned up the volume on the radio.

"You're going to have to explain that because I feel like I'm about to fall off the edge."

The edge of what? he asked.

"I don't know," I said. "Life."

Nah! Stop thinking about it, he said, grooving to the music.

"It's not that easy!" I turned down the radio and gave him my cut-the-shit look. Dad noticed I was serious now.

Alright, kiddo, look. He looked and sounded more paternal, at least for him. *There's something you need to accept. You got my face.*

"What's that mean?"

They can see it on our faces that we're not like them. We're punks and it scares them to death. They're scared of anyone who won't play their game.

"Who's they?"

Normies. Like that chick you pushed over. Like that class president who went on and on about nothing.

Dad gazed out through the pollen-tinted car window at the passing houses. While pondering his words at the next intersection, I stared directly into the red glow of the traffic light, not moving when it turned green until the guy behind us honked.

Keep pushing them over, he said. *One by one. You only need yourself.*

I wasn't convinced, but before I could press him, I looked over and saw he was gone, again. *Catch a Wave* had faded into some shitty dance song that I immediately switched off.

So I only needed myself? If this was true, I wasn't sure I wanted to be a punk anymore. I was tired of myself, tired of being a solo artist.

As I drove on through the center of town, I took stock of my options and realized I was running out of them. Once they kicked me out of the children's home, I'd be forced to live in my car until I could scrape together rent money for a room or a cheap apartment. I could put myself on someone's doorstep. But who? There was always grandma. So what if we hadn't talked in years? Isn't there a rule that grandmothers *must* take in homeless granddaughters?

And it's not like we had zero history. When mom was sober and had custody, we would visit grandma and sometimes even live in her basement. But our stays always ended with the two of them screaming at each other over something ridiculous, with mom storming out, dragging me by the arm. Mom liked to say that grandma was a drunk who hated kids.

Maybe she did, and maybe I annoyed her, but I wasn't a kid anymore and it would be better than sleeping in the Walmart parking lot.

Grandma lived on Trolley Lane, a neighborhood in the old end of town, just past the boarded up, graffiti-covered train depot where I smoked weed for the first time. As I headed in that direction, I thought about what to say to her, but nothing came to me. Once I turned onto her street, passing all the 50's style ranch houses with small, fenced in yards, lawn gnomes and bird baths, I noticed how peacefully suburban everything was, how much the walkers and people working in their gardens seemed to be enjoying the warm weather and loving life. That is until my loud piece of junk car passed them by.

When I pulled up to grandma's, something seemed off. For one thing, it was white, not yellow, and there was a Prius in the driveway, not grandma's old Buick. I could feel myself shaking, so I sat in the car for at least five minutes before I finally worked up the courage to go to the front door. As I stood on the steps, I absolutely hated myself. I hated my life and where I was at that moment. But before I had a chance to change my mind, the door opened, and I froze.

It was too late. A woman I couldn't quite see, who definitely wasn't grandma, was on the other side of the screen.

Whoever was there stared at me for a few seconds, then opened the screen door.

"Sheena? Oh my God."

I recognized her as Aunt Laurie, mom's sister whom I hadn't seen in years, looking both surprised and slightly disturbed to see me. I figured the sight of me or mom probably meant some drama or that she was going to be asked for money. She seemed baffled, and who could blame her? It was crazy how much she looked like mom with that same *I need more sleep* look in her eyes.

Embarrassed by my own presence, I gazed down at my Chuck Taylors to avoid eye contact. Being there already felt like a mistake.

"Sorry," I said, not sure why my first instinct was to apologize for simply existing, but I didn't know what else to say, and I don't think she knew what to say either. I felt her sizing me up, but it was difficult to say if she was more shocked by my being there or by the nose ring and green hair.

"Jesus, you grew fast!" She said.

"Sorry." Why the hell was I apologizing *again*?

"Last time I saw you, you were this tiny little thing," she said. "And your hair wasn't green."

I shrugged and nodded, taking her last comment as a joke.

"You're probably looking for your grandmother."

"Is she here?" I glanced-over her shoulder, into the house, expecting a small white-haired lady to appear at any moment.

After what seemed to be some soul-searching, Aunt Laurie invited me in. Without answering the question about grandma, she opened the screen door and ushered me into the living room which was filled with moving boxes and covered furniture. "We just moved in as you can see."

"You're living here now?" I asked, still wondering why I still wasn't seeing grandma.

"Yes. But we still have a ton of work to do. The new kitchen, painting, updates. It never ends."

"So you'll be living with grandma?"

"Not exactly." There was sadness in her tone.

"Oh my god, did she die?" I asked. I did *not* want to hear this. Not today.

"No, your grandmother's still with us," she said.

"Where is she?"

She couldn't have looked more disgusted. "You mean your mom never told you?"

"Told me what? I don't talk to mom," I snapped back, immediately feeling guilty about my angsty tone.

My aunt exhaled loudly and sat down on a stack of boxes. "It's complicated, but this house was passed down to me after I became grandma's legal guardian. It wasn't going to be your mom for reasons we both know about, but she got a decent chunk of money out of it. She took off somewhere right after."

"So where's grandma?"

"At Windermere."

"What's Windermere?"

"An assisted living community over on Spruce Street." She sounded guilty.

"She's in a nursing home?"

"It's an assisted living community. There's a big difference, you know. Taking care of her was becoming a full-time job. She needs around-the-clock care now."

I only half listened as she went on and on about how busy her life was and her husband always working extra hours to pay for their new mortgage. While she complained, my eyes wandered past her as vague memories about the house and the neighborhood came back to me.

"Do you know where Vonny is?" My Aunt asked. Mom's name is Veronica.

"Nope."

She kept shaking her head and sighing. The subject of mom obviously bothered my aunt deeply. It made me wonder why she brought her up.

"Now and then I'll search for her online," she said. "It's sad to see those mugshots from a few years back. I think she's up in Maine now somewhere."

I knew exactly the mugshots she was talking about. I, too, had seen them on the web. The police report said they found heroin when they pulled her over for driving all over the road.

"I told her when we were kids," my aunt said. "I said she'd get hooked. I told her over and over again. And, see, that's exactly what happened."

I had enough. "I should get going," I said, realizing I was facing another dead end.

"We were going to order some pizza if you want to stay longer," my aunt said. Her offer seemed pretty sincere, and I was starving, but I didn't have the energy to be conversational and polite. I said, "See you later," as kindly as possible before exiting the house toward my car.

"It's not fair, Sheena," my aunt declared through the screen door.

I paused. "What's not?" I asked, not turning around.

"Everything that's happened to you."

I had no idea what to say to this, so I said nothing. She wasn't wrong, but what was the point of saying it? Sick to death of *everything happening to me,* I got back in the car and gassed it down the road, pissing off the gardeners again. And the faster I drove—passing 'Class of 2018' balloons tied to practically every other mailbox announcing graduation parties that weren't for me—the more pissed I got.

My aunt was right; it *wasn't* fair, yet there I was, homeless again, and with no direction, no plan. I squeezed the wheel and felt the urge to just drive and drive, until I was out of town, out of gas, until I was far from any memory, far from anything familiar. There was nothing for me in my so-called home town now, not that there ever really was. I wanted to be anywhere else, even if it meant living in my car.

Then something my aunt said struck me. It hit me between the eyes. A large sum of money had fallen into mom's lap, and the more this sunk in, the faster I raced along the winding rural backroads. One would think any mother—even my mother—would feel obligated to help out the daughter she ditched.

Now I was driving angry, almost twice the speed limit, thinking that a little bit of help from her, even paying for a semester or two, would have been nice— if not out of love, out of guilt. But I wasn't expecting a call anytime soon.

After an hour of aimless driving, while popping the occasional Xanax, I was more depressed than angry but still pretty angry. Feeling sorry for myself was never my thing, but I couldn't help it this time. The more it all sunk in, the more convinced I was that mom owed me.

Yes, *owed*. Sure, she failed in every way as a mother. She couldn't handle it. How could she when she couldn't even handle herself? But writing a check is easy, and at least it would be something. It wouldn't erase all the hurt or cure me of my issues, but it would give me some hope, some direction. Didn't I deserve that? Why should being a music teacher seem like such an impossible dream?

That was it. No, I wasn't going to live in my crappy car in the Walmart parking lot. I decided right then and there to find her, to put myself on her doorstep with no warning. I was going to track her down and make her face me. What did I have to lose? It was a perfectly reasonable request, and for just a few grand, mom could actually do something sort of motherly for once. Sending me to college would be her penance.

This *everything happening to me* bullshit was going to stop. I was going to make something happen. I was going to take what the universe refused to give me.

The only problem was finding her. If the online mugshots were from a few years back, mom could've been anywhere by now. There was only one person I thought of who might have a clue.

Chapter Three

I always wanted to be closer to my grandmother, but she had other crap to deal with, like putting up with my alcoholic grandfather on top of living with a drug addict daughter. Though she was never the kind of grandmother who baked cookies or knitted sweaters, grandma did what she could and would even visit me at the children's home. Early in my freshman year, though, her visits stopped, and I wasn't sure why.

I didn't remember saying anything to piss her off. She just stopped coming, stopped calling, stopped being in my life. I was never mad about it because it's not like I made the effort either.

On the way to the nursing home, I remembered going there on a field trip with my sixth grade chorus to sing Christmas carols. Even as a kid, the place depressed me. It was like death's waiting room—a place you're put when no one wants you anymore. Now grandma was there, and it didn't matter that we weren't close anymore; the thought of her living there still bugged the shit out of me.

So when I finally pulled into the lot, my anxiety raged knowing I'd be seeing her in that place. But I wasn't turning around. With a little courage and a few Xanax, this was finally my chance to make something happen.

I crossed the parking lot and entered through the automatic doors. That smell hit me—that soiled-linen-hospital-smell unique to nursing homes and hospitals, a mixture of stale urine and despair. A receptionist with long red nails and dyed blonde hair signed me in and directed me toward the elevator, and when I got off on the third floor and made my way down the hallway, I cringed at the sounds of beeping machines coming from the rooms. As I walked, I felt the eyes of the staff on me who were probably wondering what this gawky teenage girl with green hair could possibly want there.

I stopped at room 302 and looked in. The lights were off and the blinds were fully drawn. The bed closest to the door was empty and perfectly made, but the sun seeping through the closed blinds was strong enough to reveal grandma, sitting up on the other bed—very still—slumped into a pile of pillows. I entered timidly and inched toward her.

My voice quivered. "Grandma?"

She turned toward me like she heard a noise but wasn't too sure. This freaked me out a little. I knew she'd look older, but she looked like a different person. Her hair, once a lovely grayish brown blend, was now pure white. Her face, once round and pink, was now caved in and pale. Her eyes, which were once sharp and aware, now seemed hollow. She squinted at me as I went closer.

Her voice cracked and sounded like she hadn't talked in weeks. "Vonny?"

I corrected her gently. "I'm Sheena, Grandma."

"Who?"

"Shee…*na*, your *grand…daughter.*" I spoke slowly and clearly, hoping for some glimmer of recognition.

"What did you do to your hair? You colored it green?"

I ran my fingers through it. "I did, Grandma. You like it?"

She glared at me. "No," she said, not sparing me in the slightest. "And what's that in your nose? Don't tell me! You didn't!"

"Yes, Grandma, I pierced my nose."

She grunted and turned back toward the window. "I thought you were in Maine or New York, or somewhere. Back for money again, I'll bet. Well, you can't take blood from a stone."

"Grandma, it's Sheena. Vonny's daughter. Your granddaughter. Do you remember me?"

Grandma looked at me suspiciously. "Don't bullshit me," she growled.

I repeated, "I'm *Sheena*," even more slowly and loudly, but it seemed I wasn't going to convince her of my existence. She was fading, clinging to scraps of memory. Whatever space I once occupied in her mind had been erased now, like I never happened.

Maybe coming here was a mistake, I thought. What was I trying to accomplish? I stood there speechless as a nurse entered with a tray. After making several frustrated attempts to feed her, the nurse gave up and left the room.

"They expect me to eat that slop?" Grandma said, pushing the tray away from her. "I wouldn't feed that gruel to a dog."

"You need to eat something, Grandma," I said.

"When there's something worth eating, I'll eat."

"You need your strength," I said.

"Stop telling me what to do! And you look like a whore, you know, with that hair." I felt like running out, but instead, I wracked my brain for fond memories, something—*anything*—to give her; a nice one involving me. But there were so few. I sat on the bed next to her.

"Do you remember Graham Lake, Grandma?" This may have been the closest thing I had to one of those 'golden childhood memories' that most people have, when mom, grandma, my Aunt Laurie and I stayed a few summer nights in a cabin by a lake. I remember swimming while mom cooked burgers over a charcoal grill. I remember a rope swing and a rocky beach. And, miraculously, I don't remember any family brawls.

"Do I remember what?" She asked. "What are you talking about, Vonny?"

I did everything I could to help her remember: "The cabin was really old with this old-fashioned sink and there was a rope swing on a tree outside. Mom and I paddled around in a canoe and you watched while sitting in a chair on the shore."

Grandma's eyes darted around like she was trying to recall it, nearly seeing it from a distance like it was across a dark room, just out of her vision.

After a moment, she gave up. "Are you on drugs again, Vonny?" She asked. "Don't lie."

I wanted to cry. "No, I'm not on drugs, Grandma." This felt like a white lie, but it really wasn't since, technically, my doctor prescribed my Xanax. Or at least he used to. Grandma shook her head and clenched her blanket.

"I shouldn't have let you quit dancing. That's when all this started, you know. That's when all the trouble began! You joined that rock group in high school and it was all downhill." She lowered her head onto the pillow.

Other than confusing me with mom, she was pretty on point. Mom's troubles, from what I've heard anyway, all started on the road when she was trying to make it big with her band. She dropped out early in her senior year after winning some regional battle of the bands in Boston which led to them touring as an opener for some headliner I never heard of while chasing the gods of music and fame. They spent a couple of months on the road, where, along the way, she decided to put a spike into her vein for the first time.

I stood there looking at grandma, feeling invisible. To her, I didn't exist. Not anymore. I whispered, "I love you," as she lay there with her back toward me. I'm not sure why I said this or how much I even meant it. I guess I did, but she couldn't have loved me. Maybe she did at one point, but how can you love someone who no longer exists in your mind? I don't think she heard what I said anyhow.

"I'm tired," she said. "I'm gonna take a nap, then you'll take me back to Trenton with you after I wake up. Right? I hate it here."

She said, "Don't leave me here," several times. "Take me to Trenton." Wherever Trenton was, it sounded familiar. I pulled the covers over her, kissed her on the head, and left quietly as she drifted to sleep.

I jumped in my car again and drove in no particular direction, feeling guilty as hell for leaving grandma alone in that place and pissed at my aunt for putting her there. But it's not like I could take her with me. With the weight of the world on me, I had to pull over for no other reason but to cry. I mean, really, really cry. For too long, I wanted to bawl my eyes out, and it was as good a time as any.

A few minutes later, I dried my eyes, took out my phone and Googled 'Veronica+Bellview+Trenton+Maine' and came across two possible addresses, one in a well-to-do section of town, one in a trailer park. After entering the most likely address into Google Maps, I hurried back to the children's home, shoved clothes into my backpack, and grabbed my guitar. After making a quick pit stop at my dealer's apartment to replenish my Xanax, I hit route 95 and headed north as the sun lowered itself into the distant hills of my home town. I looked over at the empty passenger seat, hoping to see dad.

Chapter Four

When I was a little girl and heard the morning school bus pass our apartment, I knew it was going to be another *home day*. Home days were the opposite of school days when mom stayed in bed and didn't take me to school. By the time I was in first grade, it was happening almost every day. For most kids, this would be a dream come true, but it was a nightmare for me.

It's not like mom did anything with me at home; she just slept all day because she was 'sick'. And because I was absent so often, I always felt like the new girl at school, never around enough to make friends. The teacher always looked surprised to see me when I stumbled into the classroom late with messy hair, wearing old clothes that barely fitted me. So, as I lay in bed on one particular morning, knowing I had another long, boring home day ahead of me, I couldn't stop myself from crying into my pillow.

I couldn't understand why mom was always so sick. Then the phone rang.

As usual, it was the school secretary, reporting my absence on the answering machine, pointing out the number of absences up to that point. *Twenty-three.* I wanted to pick up and tell her it wasn't my fault, that I really wanted to be in school, and that I would take the bus if mom would let me go. I wanted to tell her I didn't care about not having nice clothes or packed lunches with special notes from mom inside; I still wanted to go.

I wanted friends. I wanted to know my teacher and I wanted her to like me. Most of all, I wanted someone to help us.

This time, on what was my fifth home day in a row, I felt desperate enough to pick up, so I slipped out of bed after the second ring and went into the kitchen, passing mom's slightly open door. When the phone rang a third time, I picked up the cordless phone and peeped into mom's bedroom. I nearly answered but froze when I saw mom slumped over the side of the bed, throwing up into a small trash can.

She was gagging, so I dropped the phone and rushed into her room. I stood at the foot of her bed, barely noticing the secretary's voice on the answering machine, and watched in horror, wondering what on earth was making my mother so sick.

Mom wiped her mouth and looked up with half-closed eyes. "Can you get my bag?" She said with barely enough energy to get the words out.

"Why are you sick, Mom?" I asked.

"Sheena, my bag."

"You need to go to the doctor," I said.

"It's fine. I just need some medicine," she said.

"Mom…"

"Now, Sheena…please!"

I turned around and began my routine search for mom's bag, which was a worn-out, brown satchel that looked a hundred years old. It was where she kept her medicine, and it was always my job to find it, especially on home days. I searched in the usual spots: the TV room, between the couch cushions, under piles of clothes, but it was nowhere to be seen. Not wanting mom to feel sick for another second, I scoured the bathroom, next to the toilet, even behind the shower curtain and in the hamper—no spot was too random—but I still couldn't find it.

Predictably, mom started moaning about how long I was taking. Then, by sheer random luck, I noticed the bag strap poking out from behind the couch pillows. Dragging the satchel, I sprinted into mom's bedroom, so she'd get her medicine and feel better. I picked it up with both hands and held it toward her, proudly. Without looking me in the eye or thanking me, mom ripped the satchel out of my hands. She was in an awful mood but I stayed anyway, watching as she pushed herself up slowly. She paused and looked at me.

"Privacy, please," she said.

I looked at her, confused as to why she wanted to be alone. It's not like she was getting dressed or using the bathroom. She was only taking her medicine.

"Sheena…" she said, nodding toward the door.

She ordered me to shut the door as I left, so I did, watching her until the door was closed. There would be nothing to do that day, so I went into my own bedroom, sat down on my bed, and stared at nothing and tried to think about nothing. Home days were just that. Nothing. The next day was pretty much a repeat, only I had an easier time finding her bag. For some reason, I grew really tired later in the morning and fell asleep on the couch.

A couple of hours later, I was awoken by the sound of the school bus driving by my apartment. It was a warm day, so the windows were wide open, and I could hear its loud engine and brakes slowing it down as it came to a stop just down the street. I watched from a distance, like so many times before, as kids from school hopped off the bus. Some looked my age and seemed happier than I had ever felt, giddy to see their moms and dads waiting for them. Mom never let me wander down that busy street alone, and because she was never up at that time, the bus wasn't an option.

As the bus drove away, I had a bright idea.

That night, after dinner—which was Cheerios and milk that tasted old—I found a nearly clean shirt and a pair of jeans and draped them over the reading chair in my room. After some rummaging, I was able to find my old Hello Kitty alarm clock and was surprised but thrilled to find the batteries still working. I was even able to figure out how to set it for 7 am. At that point, I didn't care. I was going to school.

I could barely sleep that night. I was nervous about making the bus, getting those awkward stares from classmates who had forgotten who I was. But I was mostly nervous about leaving mom by herself. Would she get sick again? Would she be able to find her medicine? The next morning, after brushing my hair and getting dressed, I found her satchel and tiptoed into her room. After placing it on the pillow next to her head, I kissed her cheek, strapped on my backpack, and tiptoed out of the apartment.

Within fifteen minutes, I was on the bus, heading to school, feeling like a normal kid. Sure, I was defying mom, but I also knew there was a good chance she'd never find out.

And I was right…at least for a while. For an entire week, I was able to get myself up and ready and make the bus. Soon, after some extra help from my teacher, I understood just about everything that was going on in class—even the math lessons. At lunch, two girls let me sit with them, and at recess, they included me in their games of tag and four square. Everything was going so well, which is why I had an awful sneaky feeling in my stomach that it wouldn't last.

I knew my luck was running out when I caught a sideways look from a mother at the bus stop. It was the kind of judgmental glare that said 'What sort of mother lets her kid walk home alone?' She looked familiar, and I'm pretty sure she called home that afternoon because mom was waiting for me at the bus stop at drop-off, and she didn't look happy. Standing apart from the others, wearing a black t-shirt and pajama bottoms, she had her arms crossed as I shuffled toward her, caught in the act. I was disappointed in myself for feeling embarrassed by how she looked and less afraid of how much trouble I was in.

She dragged me home by the arm without a word but immediately started yelling the minute we were back in our apartment.

"How long have you been taking the bus?" She asked.

I shrugged.

"Answer me!" She demanded.

"I don't know," I said, which was a truthful answer.

"You can't walk yourself to the bus stop. Do you know how dangerous that road is?"

"Why won't you go with me?" I asked staring straight into her eyes. "Walk with me."

"I'm perfectly capable of driving you to school."

"I always miss school."

Mom paused and for a moment was speechless. She knew I was right. She knew my defiance was mostly her doing, not mine. Still, she had to make an excuse.

"I've been sick, Sheena. I'm trying to get better. I really am. You need to trust me." I stared at the floor, trying to make sense of a seemingly impossible situation. Silence was my only defense.

Mom sat on the laundry covered couch. "Just give me a little time to get better, okay? I'll be better about getting you to school. I promise."

"Tomorrow?"

Mom had to think about it. Finally, she said, "Sure. Tomorrow is good."

Later that evening, mom was in a really great mood, chatting about everything, playing music on the stereo; she even made mac and cheese for dinner. After cleaning up and doing the dishes, she helped me with my Language Arts homework and picked out my outfit for the next school day— a nice denim dress with striped leggings. She even dug out a nice pair of slip-on shoes I had forgotten about. Everything was perfect and I was more excited than ever to go to school.

Around 9 pm, I got into my pajamas and said goodnight to mom. And even though she said she'd wake me in the morning, I still felt the urge to set my Hello Kitty clock. But for some reason, I just didn't. I didn't want to. I chose to believe her. With my hand on the button, I laid there thinking—why should I? Don't I trust her? She's feeling so much better tonight.

The way things are going, she might even make me breakfast in the morning. Taking mom at her word, I pulled my hand away from the alarm clock, turned over and went to sleep.

The next morning, I woke up with an incredible feeling. With my eyes still closed, I thought about my nicely ironed outfit, my cool shoes, and my new friends at school. But as I opened my eyes and heard the bus pass our apartment, my heart sank. I didn't hear mom at all. I didn't smell breakfast cooking. I looked at my clock and realized it was going to be another home day. Nothing had changed.

I got up and went to mom's bedroom, pushed open the door which creaked loudly. She woke up.

"Shit!" Mom sat up. "What time is it?" I stood there, silent.

Mom glanced at her phone then dropped back down on to the bed. She was a different person than she was the night before. It's like she wasn't fully there with me.

"Sheena…" she whimpered, like it was too exhausting to even breathe.

I felt too angry to answer her. At that moment, I didn't care if she was sick. How can you be too sick to be a mom? Too sick to love your kid?

"Sheena?" She repeated.

I still didn't answer. I didn't care enough. If she was so sick, why wasn't she in the hospital? Maybe I should call an ambulance. But who would take care of me? Did it matter?

Mom shifted in her bed. "Get my medicine, Sheena."

I didn't move. What if I didn't get it? Would she die? I didn't want her to but maybe she'd go to the hospital and get better. Maybe she'd get new medicine that worked because the kind she had wasn't working. This medicine sucked.

"Now, Sheena!" She screamed. I jumped and looked in all the usual places. This time, her satchel was in the kitchen on the counter next to the coffee maker. But in my haste, I picked it up from the wrong end and nearly everything inside dumped out onto the counter and the floor—her keys, gum, cigarettes, and a bunch of loose change; but there was something else, something I only saw on visits to the doctors. I only knew them as *shots*.

I hated shots. I remember thinking as I put everything back into the purse that mom must have been *really* sick if she was giving herself shots at home.

Chapter Five

Normally, I'd be listening to something loud and crazy on a road trip to get my mind off things—Sex Pistols, Black Flag, maybe—but this wasn't a normal road trip at all, and I needed the long silence to think about what I was going to say to mom and how I was going to say it. Which version of me was I going to show her? The same angry, bitter girl who bulldozed that chick at graduation? Or maybe the sad girl who cries herself to sleep? Maybe this time mom needed to see both of me.

Another worry was my piece of shit car, a Honda Accord on its last leg with nearly 200,000 miles. The thing drove like it could explode at any moment, and I had little money to fix it unless it involved duct tape. But making it to Trenton was all I cared about. If I had to crawl, I was going to face mom; I was getting what was owed to me, and I felt absolutely no shame about it.

It was only after an hour of driving, while crossing the long chain-bridge into Maine, that I was finally able to calm down. Road trips always had this effect on me. With a clear head, I analyzed this insane thing I was doing, and for the first time in days, I felt a smile. I felt totally free, like I was finally taking control of life, finally doing *something*. I was so elated that I didn't even notice the Xanax wearing off. This feeling soon gave way to something I hadn't felt in some time—creative inspiration.

Despite everything, it still came in waves, and when it did, I would run to my guitar no matter where I was because I knew it wouldn't last, and that soon, life would stop being fun again. Sometimes I'd ride the wave long enough to actually write a song. Knowing how rare this was, I had to go somewhere to play my music. It was like I had no choice. Better still, I wanted more than anything to share it—to perform.

So without hesitation, and a smile still plastered across my face, I took the next exit to downtown Portland and followed the signs that led me to an Old

Port district and parked in a public lot. Trembling with excitement that bordered on manic, I grabbed my guitar from the backseat and headed toward the waterfront.

It was a warm night. The cobblestone streets were filled with roaming tourists popping in and out of shops and bars, many were enjoying ice cream cones, watching street performers, or just taking in the balminess of a summer dusk. The smell of the harbor breeze wafting past the harbor side restaurants made me crave seafood or anything deep fried. It was exhilarating to feel almost normal and to be in a place so full of life and to want to be a part of it all in some way—even on borrowed time, before my good mood dissolved back into its usual darkness.

After some wandering, I found a pleasant spot down by the pier, far enough away from the other street musicians, under a dock light. I placed my guitar case on a bench and took out my instrument. An old friend—my *only* friend— as I strapped it around me and held it close, touching the strings with my coarse finger tips.

As day fell into night, I strummed the opening chords to *Asleep* by The Smiths, then, after some brief awkwardness, I cleared my throat and began to sing. My voice was shaky at first, but in no time, it became free and unrestrained. Fully me. As I eased into the next verse, tourists started to gather and listen; some even tossed money into my case. It had been over a year since I played in front of people—at an open mic at school—but as more people formed around me, I remembered how much I had missed it.

Invigorated by the applause and feeling nothing short of euphoric, I played *The Exploding Boy* by The Cure. After more applause and a third song, which was *Perfect Day* by Lou Reed, I felt brave enough to sing my most recent original, a song I wrote sitting on my bed at the children's home called 'Longing'. By the second verse, I was totally into it, even singing with my eyes closed, a gesture I always hated. But I didn't care; it was so good to be heard again.

And from what I could tell, the small crowd seemed to like me.

After my final song, I lowered the guitar and smiled sheepishly as everyone clapped and wandered off. I gathered the money from my guitar case—which looked to be over $50—and shoved it all into my pocket. Sensing that someone was still there watching me, I glanced up and saw this cute guy standing under the lamp, grinning. He was a little older than me, so I guess you could say I was a bit creeped out.

He didn't say anything, so I tilted my head. "Ummm, is this the part where you say something?"

"You're really, really good." The guy was hot, for sure, but in an offbeat, bohemian kind of way. More Paris than Portland, with this thick quaff of black hair, jeans, and a black t-shirt.

I stood up. "I'm really not that good, but thanks anyway. It's nice of you to lie," I said with a little edge in my voice in order to keep myself from blushing.

"No lie!" His voice was intelligent, warm and deep. "Is that guitar a Martin?" He asked.

"That's what it says on the case."

"What a beautiful instrument! Vintage. Great tone."

"I take it you play?" I asked coolly, pretending I didn't care either way.

He smiled. "A little bit. I'm no James Taylor. Do you mind?" He reached for my guitar.

"So this is where you show off and make me look bad, right?" I said, handing it over.

"Nah. This is where I prove that I have stone hands." He laughed, handling my guitar like it was a holy relic. "This is an amazing guitar. It's gotta be worth, I don't know, five-grand at least."

"Like I'd ever sell it."

"Of course not. You keep something this beautiful forever."

For some reason, I giggled and even snorted, even though nothing was really funny. For someone who tried to play it cool, I could feel myself getting uncontrollably red. And it wasn't just his looks. It was more about how he talked and carried himself. He was smooth, but not in a fake way. Unlike me, this guy seemed comfortable with who he was.

And as an added bonus, he played the guitar beautifully, plucking notes like a traditional folk singer. His hands were definitely not stone.

He looked up. "Do you perform often? Have a demo or mix tape?"

I laughed. "No!"

"Why is that funny?"

"Mix tape? Why bother?"

"Why bother?" He repeated with a hint of outrage.

"Anyone with an iPhone can hear a million singers way better than I am in two clicks on YouTube. So, yeah, why bother?" This was completely idiotic and I knew it. But deflecting compliments was a true talent and an involuntary reaction.

He laughed. "YouTube? Are you serious? I prefer real people." *Real people.* Me too, I thought as he continued to pluck and strum.

"I've never seen you around here," he said.

"That's because I'm never around here."

"Where are you from then?"

"Nowhere special."

"Oh, so you're on tour!"

"I guess you can say I need the money."

He smiled, stood up, and handed the guitar back. "Are you busy?"

"Now?"

"Yes, now!" He laughed.

I froze. Was he actually expressing interest in *me*? Wide-eyed, unable to utter a word, I stood there holding the guitar. He leaned in, waiting for my answer.

Finally, he said, "This is the part where you answer the question."

"Yes—I mean, no. I'm not...busy at...uh, this precise moment. Now." I was stammering like hell.

"If you're looking for something to do, there's this folk band playing at the Pour House on Lime Street at 8:00."

Of course, I wanted to go with him to wherever, but I hesitated, realizing how late it was and how I had hung around longer than I really wanted to. Then I thought about it: there was no way I'd get to mom's before 11:00, even if I left at that moment. Was I really going to ambush her out at that hour? Leaving the next morning seemed to make more sense.

"Yeah, okay, I guess. Why not?" I said, trying not to seem overly excited, even though I was ecstatic.

"Great! They're a pretty good band. Four old hippies who can still jam. And, hey, if you don't like them, we can leave...watch some singers on YouTube."

I picked up my guitar case and followed this guy across the pier and down a few side streets until we were at the center of the Old Port. After all the polite banter, I finally learned his name was Tim, a former U Maine art student who dropped out after finding the experience 'too restricting'.

"College wasn't my scene. I was in front of a computer screen more than in front of a canvas. Who needs that shit?"

The more he talked, the more I realized he wasn't the kind of guy you'd ever meet in a town where I lived, or used to live. Everything he said was interesting and unconventional.

"Their program was all about commercial art and making money," he said. "Using art to sell shit. No, thanks."

"We all need money, right?" I said, feeling a little guilty, considering the reason for my trip was to get money.

He shrugged. "It depends on what you want. I get money here and there for doing murals or making caricatures down on the docks for tourists when I'm desperate. I get by. The trick is knowing what you can do without."

I paused and pondered what he just said. He was absolutely right, and I felt like an idiot.

He smiled at me and said, "I probably sound crazy."

"Nah. Well, maybe a little." I smiled back.

As if struck by a sudden idea, Tim took my hand and led me down Market Street and into a municipal parking lot. "Look," he said, pointing to the far end of the lot. "That's home for me." What he meant by home was an old gray pickup truck with one of those small pop-up campers in the back. "Give me that over a cookie-cutter mansion any day, and you can keep the thirty-year mortgage that comes with it."

I smiled at him and lowered my guard even more. "Pretty cool," I said.

Then he got a little too serious for me and said, "You gotta live on your own terms, not society's terms."

"Thanks for the advice, Dr. Phil," I joked.

He blushed and laughed again. "Sorry. I didn't mean to get preachy. I'm really the last person to give advice."

"Forget it," I said. "You're not saying anything I don't agree with. Actually, life on my terms is exactly what I'm going for—for once. It's why I'm on the road."

He nodded. "That's great, right on. If you don't mind my asking, what…"

"What am I doing here?"

"I hope I'm not being intrusive."

"You definitely are…"

He laughed nervously. "Are you always this punchy?"

"Only when I'm nervous, which is most of the time and especially now. I'm on my way to see my mother for the first time in five years."

"Whoa. No shit?"

"Yeah, no shit." I wasn't really sure why I was telling him any of this. The guy could be a serial killer for all I knew. But when you're like me, someone who constantly keeps everything inside, it's easy to suddenly spill everything, especially when someone seems to care.

"Sorry," he said, speaking in a softer, more sincere voice. "I didn't mean to stick my nose in your business."

"I don't mind."

We took our time, making our way across the waterfront district, talking about art, politics, and even God at one point; it was almost embarrassing how much we agreed on things. We were so deep in conversation that I forgot all about seeing a hippie band at some coffee house. And to be honest, I didn't care if we just kept walking and talking all night and blew off the hippies.

When we were almost there, Tim stopped like he had some sort of epiphany. "If I show you something, a secret," he said, "do you promise not to tell anyone?"

For the second time that night, I froze and looked at him awkwardly. I was afraid to answer, wondering if this was when he brings out the axe or reveals he's a perv or that his truck is a meth lab.

"Trust me," he said, taking my hand, leading me down a narrow street that cuts between two buildings. Why I followed him, I can't really say, but he soon stopped in the most shadowy area with no streetlights and pointed at the side of an old brick building.

"Check that out," he said, grinning.

It was too dark, so he took out his lighter and produced a soft glow that reflected off the stone wall. Squinting, I saw a painting. I took a closer look; it was a painted mural of a homeless man on a park bench covered in newspapers.

"You painted this?" I asked, truly impressed at the detail.

"Yeah, you dig it?" He asked, clearly proud of his work and for good reason. "Did you notice the newspapers?" He moved the lighter closer to the wall and told me to read the headlines, which I did, realizing his work was a clear social statement: 'DOW SURGES', 'NEW WAR, NEW JOBS'. It wasn't a subtle message but it was a powerful one. Mostly, I was truly impressed with the artwork, and I guess you could say I was impressed with Tim, too.

Tim lit a cigarette. "The cops call that graffiti," he said, exhaling smoke. "It pisses people off. But shouldn't all art do that?"

He offered me a cigarette, which I took, and lit it for me. "It's great," I said. "I really like it."

"I'm glad," he said. "Can't learn that on a computer in college."

I nodded.

Five minutes later, we were in an artsy coffee bar listening to an acoustic set by a band called Indigo Child who weren't that bad for a gang of old stoners. Tim and I chatted between songs, sipping coffee and shamelessly flirting. We were probably a big distraction but we were too absorbed in each other to care. Then, after about an hour, we got bored with the music and left.

As we wandered again through town, I realized that if things kept going like this, I'd be spending the night in Portland, at least this was the vibe I was getting. So it was no surprise when I found myself an hour later sitting close to Tim on the public beach, watching the waves roll in and out. Not once did he try to get in my pants. It seemed he only wanted to be with me and nothing more, which was something I wasn't used to when it came to guys.

And just when I thought the night couldn't get any better, Tim reached for my guitar and sang *Sleep* by The Smiths, complete with a kick-ass Morrissey impression. Sure, the whole thing was a little corny, but I didn't mind; it was all part of me letting my guard down. I just relaxed, lowered my head on his shoulders, and let it all happen. By the third verse, I was asleep.

The first thing I heard when I woke was the sound of the waves. I didn't open my eyes right away, but the sun penetrating my eyelids told me it was morning. My night with Tim was already in my head, and for the first time in who knows how long, it felt good to wake up; it felt good because I knew he was the kind of guy who would still be there, next to me, once I opened my eyes.

But I kept them closed for a bit, taking in this newness, listening to the waves crash, thinking of how cool it was to feel a connection to someone, to feel something real.

But when I fully opened my eyes and rubbed away the sleep and sunlight, I saw, and I saw it with a near-instant acceptance, like I knew it was coming, it had to, that I was alone. I looked around, then stood. There was no one else, just an older couple walking their dog along the beach. I wanted to deny it, to believe Tim had snuck away early to surprise me with coffee and scones or maybe flowers. But I knew Tim was about to be added to my list of disappointments. One of many, so what's one more?

Normally, I wouldn't allow myself to care too much. But it was different this time. This one hurt, and it hurt infinitely worse when I saw that my guitar was also gone. In a panic, I jumped up and looked around, frantically. Nothing. There was no sign of it. A few feet away, written in the sand, a message confirmed my fear:

Sorry, I'm desperate.

I was too pissed off to be hurt and wanted badly to punch something or someone. My guitar was my rock, the one thing I could turn to when things got really shitty. And just like that, it was gone. I kicked sand everywhere. The couple walking their dog stared as I sprinted up the walkway and onto the street. In two minutes, I was in the Old Port district with my head on a swivel, like some raving lunatic.

With my heart racing, I ran to the old municipal lot, but of course, his truck was gone. I felt like an idiot, a total fool. Did I really think it would be there?

You don't rip off a rare $5,000 instrument and hang around. Then, in my last act of desperation, I returned to the coffee shop from the night before, which had just opened for the day. A young woman was milling around, placing muffins in the display case as I stormed to the counter, breathless. She looked up, startled. She knew I wasn't there for muffins.

"Are you okay?" She asked, wide-eyed.

"So I was here last night with this guy—long hair, unshaven. He seemed to know some of the employees here."

Her expression turned sour. "I remember you. You sat over there." She pointed at the exact table.

"Yeah, yeah. Do you know the guy I was with?"

Her eyes rolled as she continued to arrange the baked goods. "Don't get me started with that guy. Sorry if you're into him. But if I had the chance to talk to you alone last night, I would have warned you about that asshole. Again, sorry if he's like a boyfriend or whatever, but I'm not holding back."

"Warn me about what?" I asked. "Do you know where I can find him? Do you know his last name?"

"His name changes all the time. He was Carl this time last year when I lent him $100 that I never got back. I stopped chasing him because I want nothing to do with that loser."

I just stared at her blankly.

But her rant wasn't over. "The douche comes around every few months and leeches off someone. Wait…you didn't give him money, did you?"

I closed my eyes and shook my head. "He stole my fucking guitar." I wanted to scream, cry, and punch a hole in the display case. My pain and anger must have been obvious as my face was burning and hot tears were rolling off my face.

Looking genuinely sorry for me, she came from behind the counter and touched my shoulder. "Shit, really? That totally sucks, for real. Now I feel guilty not telling you."

"Don't worry about it," I said running my hand through my hair. "I'm the idiot who decided to trust some guy I just met."

"I get it. He's nice looking, seems cool at first. He talks a good game. That's his method, ya know."

I wiped away my tears. "And no one knows who he is—like really is? Didn't he go to college around here?"

Her face turned really sympathetic now, like the way guidance counselors always looked at me. "He gave you the art college routine? He used that one on me. He showed you the third rate Banksy mural over on Milk Street, right? The homeless guy with all the newspapers?"

I nodded, slowly. I was the world's biggest idiot.

"That's not his work. One of the real art students did it."

"Fuck," I said, and what else was there to say? For someone who grew up literally unable to trust anyone, why the hell did I start then? Did I really want something new and real to happen this badly? How could I not detect such an obvious con artist?

"This really blows," she said lifting her notepad and pen. "Why don't you leave your number, and if that piece of shit comes around again, I'll text you. Maybe you can press charges or something. I'd love to see that guy in cuffs."

I gave her my number and left with my head low and my feet dragging, like I was just booed off the stage. The trouble with being a solo performer like me is that you don't have anyone to back you up when things go wrong.

After a slow, tortuous prowl through town, I found my car and drove off with no intention whatsoever of stopping until I got to Trenton. I floored it, blasted dad's music, popped two Xans, and was now more determined than ever to unload on my mother. With my best punk rock sneer, I stared ahead at the lonely highway in front of me, wondering if everyone in this world was made of stone.

39 Ivers, Pierced Girls.

Chapter Six

I pushed through the new morning along the misty highway, stopping only once to pee. The deeper into Maine I drove, the more I wondered if I was being brave or ridiculous. Would I even find her? People like mom are usually drifters, always on the move. If shit was really bad—like if she had been recently evicted or let out of jail—she could have been living out of her car (if she had one) or squatting in some drug den with twenty other junkies like her. I've been with her in both situations.

But if things were looking up for her—if she had a job or was in one of her pseudo-rehab phases—she could be renting a room or living in some church lady's basement. With mom, everything was temporary, good situations were fragile. But if my aunt was telling the truth—and why would she lie—mom had cash and could've been living in her own apartment by now. Of course, there was the chance that every cent was gone already, all of it spent on her 'medicine'.

While parked in some seedy rest stop, after a winding stretch lined with moose crossing signs, I pulled out my phone and searched again for my mother's address. As usual, her mugshots came up first, one that was ten years old and one from the year before. The more recent of the two was posted on a Trenton Police Department Facebook page, which seemed like public shaming to me, the modern equivalent of locking a prisoner in stocks.

The comments below infuriated me most. Mom was no saint but did she deserve to be belittled publicly by random people who didn't even know her, who called 'scum' and 'a waste of oxygen'?

One particular comment caught my attention. It said: 'pure trailer trash. Lives over in the Oak Grove trailer park they should shut down. drug-infested rat hole lock her up!'

I looked up Oak Grove and saw it was only an hour away with a 7:08 am arrival time, according to Google Maps. The impulsive psycho in me wanted to arrive as early as possible just so I could pound on her door with *We're a Happy Family* by the Ramones blaring on my car stereo.

I imagined her disbelief. 'Hello, mother dearest. Did you make me eggs?' But as much as I wanted to lash out, to make some dramatic statement, I figured a more subtle approach would better serve my cause—which, to be honest—was to get money. Hoping to calm myself, I took another Xanax and pulled back onto the highway.

An hour later, I took the Trenton ramp. With sweat dripping under my leather jacket and sliding down my spine, I felt my courage was fading, but I wasn't turning back now. I was making this happen, regardless of how I felt. Still, the thought of seeing mom for the first time in years was getting too real, so I pulled into the empty parking lot of some lobster pound to just calm down, to force myself to stop shaking. I parked and took deep breaths as an old man dumped mounds of lobsters into a massive steaming pot. Soon I was reciting what I could say:

"Hey, Mom. Can't hide now, can you?" (*Nah. Too aggressive.*)

"I know you have money!" (*No. Too direct.*)

"I really need you, Mom." (*Too…needy?*)

But as the old man had dumped his sixth lobster trap, I thought, *screw it. Whatever I blurt out will be right. And if nothing comes to me, maybe saying nothing will say everything.* After a few more deep breaths, I drove and merged back onto the coastal road and headed northbound through thick patches of fog rolling off the ocean.

The farther I drove, the harder it was to picture mom living in a place so quaint, a town stuck in the past with its ma and pa shops, antique stores, and old home days. It was like being in a Maine postcard…that is until Google took me down a narrow dirt motorway toward a wooded shore. After a few bends in the road, I saw a rusted sign telling me I was at Oak Grove trailer park. I was moments away from seeing her again, moments away from something I expected to be unbearably surreal, and moments away from facing her.

Noticing a mailbox kiosk, I parked and jumped out to scan the names. I was in luck: *Vonny B.* number 18. After another half-mile on this bumpy dirt road—passing 14, then 16—I found trailer 18. Practically falling apart, the thing had clutter all around it: empty kegs, scraps of plywood, crappy lawn chairs, and the lawn hadn't been mowed in months. I pulled closer and parked on the road at a safe distance.

I stepped out, practically convulsing, as I clenched my pill bottle in my pocket for comfort. Seeing her mugshot was hard enough, so how the hell was I going to face her now? I wanted to get back in the car, but something kept me going toward that screen door, like I was caught in a tractor beam. Would she even recognize me? Would she even open the door? Would she even be in?

Getting closer, I knocked these thoughts out of my mind, taking deep breaths with every step. But it was no use—my heart was thumping like a punk rock bass. I needed to be angry again, and I tried to channel my adrenaline into rage; but instead, I felt like a scared little girl, dragging her blanket toward mommy's room after a bad dream.

I approached the door and listened for any sign of life. The blankets draped on the other side of the windows reminded me of how much mom hated sunlight and how it was still too early. But I knocked anyway—timidly at first, then harder. Still, I heard nothing, just the tinkling from a neighbor's wind chimes. I held my breath and knocked again, louder this time with a clenched fist.

Finally, I heard an inside door open and the floor creak. Someone was up, so I waited and listened as footsteps came closer. At that moment, I regretted everything and wanted to take it all back. I wanted to run, to forget my dumb scheme. But as I turned to leave, as the door opened behind me, I tripped over my own feet and fell face down onto the driveway.

Mortified, I didn't move, like I was playing dead.

"Why the hell are you knocking this early! Who are you?" It was a raspy woman's voice, a chain-smoker's voice. I knew it was mom. "We're out of everything anyway," she said. "Try next week, but call Jim first for fuck's sake."

I got up and turned slowly, ashamed to show my face. After wiping dirt off my legs, I lifted my head and shrugged like I was sorry to be there. But why was I sorry all of a sudden? I wanted *her* to be sorry, but she didn't seem to even recognize me. Was it the dyed hair? The nose ring? The dark eye-shadow? But I recognized *her* alright, though she looked so much older now with hair that was more gray than black.

Her sunken eyes were surrounded by dark circles. But behind all the lines and all the creases in her face, some beauty remained. She was still very much mom.

It took her a few moments but when it dawned on her, she covered her mouth and squinted like her eyes were deceiving her. In disbelief, she muttered 'Holy shit' under her breath and said my name. Of course she was shocked. How could she have been anything else? I was from a past life, and the last person she thought she'd see on the doorstep of her trailer that morning.

I wanted to scream at her but made it stay down deep in my insides. Despite all the pent-up rage, I could only manage a meek little "Hi, Mom." This was not the plan.

What followed was the most awkward silence of my life as we continued to stare at each other with nothing and absolutely everything to say. Her hand was still over her mouth, my expression was blank and cold. Wasn't it her turn to talk now? Something? *Anything?* I obviously wasn't expecting her to throw her arms around me—not that I wanted that—but wasn't it on her to make the next move, to make me feel like this wasn't the last place on earth I should be?

Finally, once convinced I wasn't a hallucination, she simply said, "Fuck! You look just like your father."

This observation, topped off with an obscenity, was beyond strange at that moment, but I was glad she wasn't completely horrified to see me.

"If you say so," I said.

"I love your hair," she said, still staring like I was just beamed down from another planet.

Her gawking went on and on and on, and I was getting kind of annoyed.

"So…what now?" I asked.

After fumbling for a cigarette, she lit one and shook her head. "Sorry. I'm just completely…"

"Completely what?" I asked.

"Completely…I don't know…surprised. This is like a total mind-fuck."

I peered at her. "A mind-fuck?"

"Shit, I don't know…" Then, out of nowhere, with her cigarette hanging in her mouth, she hugged me. This threw me off and was probably why I kept stiff and didn't take my hands out of my pockets. Or maybe I just forgot what a hug felt like.

She released me from the hug and said, "Shit, girl, it's been…a long time. Too long."

"I guess you can say that."

"Like four years, right?"

"Like five."

"Jesus," she said as it all sunk in. "You know, I've been meaning to call and visit…"

"Too busy?" I asked, looking around at her cluttered yard.

"I understand if you don't believe that."

"I'm good at being skeptical by now as you might imagine."

"I was, you know, waiting for the right time."

"My high school graduation might have been the right time."

I knew she wasn't going to be thrilled about being ambushed like this, but the more I spoke, the more uncomfortable she looked. She kept scratching her arms, leaving red streaks across her tattoos. She must've felt caught, exposed. I guess I was like a mirror, forcing her to look at herself. And how the hell could she be happy with what she was seeing?

"You graduated? No shit?" She said with mild enthusiasm.

"Yeah, no shit."

"Jesus, time just flies by, and then…" she trailed off with a mumble.

"And then what?"

"I don't know. You die, right?" For some reason, she cracked herself up with this, but her laughter quickly turned into a coughing fit.

More silence.

"I can't believe I'm looking at my girl right now," she said, changing the subject.

"Are you gonna invite me in?" I asked.

She dropped the cigarette and rubbed it out under her flip-flop. I wasn't sure why my simple request made her nervous. "Yeah, yeah, right, definite, sure. But, uh, can you give me like one minute? No, two minutes! Then you can come inside, and we'll talk, okay? I'm sure we have so a lot to say to each other."

I gave a whatever shrug. I hated how she spoke to me like I was some old acquaintance and not her daughter.

"Stay here," she said. "Let me straighten up a little first, okay?"

She disappeared inside, closing both doors behind her. I then heard drawers and cabinets opening and shutting. I knew she was hiding her 'medicine' and all related accessories, as though I hadn't seen it all before.

I waited impatiently for about five minutes before she reappeared, out of breath, hair pulled back in a crooked ponytail. "Sorry about that. I think we're ready for company now," she said, holding the door open for me.

We? I wondered who else was there. I followed her in and was surprised to see that, despite her efforts, clutter was still everywhere, unfolded laundry draped on dated furniture, dirty dishes stacked up in the kitchen sink, and there were cigarette holes in the carpet.

I could tell mom was a little embarrassed. "Not exactly a showroom, I know," she said.

"We had people over last night and didn't have a chance to clean up. Not that I'm Martha Stewart or anything."

The whole place looked dated, stuck in the 80s. But what really threw me were all the framed posters of heavy metal bands, like Poison and Motley Crue. None of it had mom's stamp; it looked more like a bachelor pad circa 1984.

"You can sit if you want," she said.

I sat down on an old love seat that smelled like an ashtray.

"You want a beer or something?" I shot her a funny look.

"Oh, right. Jesus. You're not old enough, right? Still, I can't believe how fast you grew up."

"I went the same speed as everyone," I said.

She took a seat at the small kitchen table across the room and fired up another smoke.

"Please say you're not here to give me bad news or anything," she said.

"Bad news?"

"You're not going to tell me someone died, like grandma or anyone else?"

"No."

"So everyone's alive?"

"I guess. How would I know?"

Mom nodded then paused. She probably wanted me to get to the point of my visit, but I really didn't feel like going there yet.

"So…you graduated, huh?" She asked when she realized I wasn't going to explain myself.

"Yup. Yesterday."

She smiled and looked me up and down. "My own kid, a high school grad," she said. "Shit, now you're more educated than me."

It was so weird hearing her say things like 'my own kid' as though she cared about me in the slightest. There's no way she cared, so why was she saying it? Was it because I was right there in front of her? Was it a way of protecting herself? Whatever the reason, I was getting pissed off by the charade.

"It would've been great to be there, Sheena, to see you graduate, really," she said.

I crossed my arms and looked away. "Bullshit," I said, more or less mumbling it, unable to hold back any longer. Apparently, I was going with brutal honesty now.

Mom slouched down more in her chair and started scratching both upper arms at the same time. "You could've invited me, you know."

"Bullshit!" I repeated, a bit louder this time. "Why should a kid have to invite her mom to her high school graduation?"

"How could I have known about it?"

"By giving a shit."

She got quiet, clearly unsure of what to say next. "Is this why you came, Sheena? To make me feel like a shithead? I am fully aware of that." She seemed genuinely hurt, not pissed off at my bitchiness. This impressed me, but only a little.

It still didn't feel quite right to bring up college at that moment, so I lied a little: "I really don't know why I came to be honest."

We both looked around the room. A breeze came in from the outside, bringing with it the smell of the sea.

All of a sudden, just when the silence became unbearable, mom jumped up. "Breakfast!" She exclaimed. Her eyes had a slightly crazed look.

"What?" I asked, totally confused.

"Maybe you came here for breakfast! I know this place."

"Uh…okay." This was completely random but I went with it.

As though in a rush, she threw on a black hoodie from the couch armrest. "You don't mind driving, right?" She asked, already heading out the door and toward my car.

I said, "Um…yeah…sure," and followed her.

As we drove away from the trailer park, along the shore road, she yammered on—in an almost stream-of-consciousness way—about the recent heatwave, the family in the next trailer, and many other random gripes.

Eventually, she directed me a few miles down the road to a local diner by the water called The Sea Witch where we got out and entered, turning many heads in our direction like the circus was in town.

Though it was in the middle of the breakfast rush, with waitresses carrying full trays, zig-zagging everywhere, we found a small table and were immediately served cups of coffee. As we sipped, she started asking me about what music I was into and if I stuck with guitar.

"Yeah, I still play," I said.

"That's so great!" She said. "Music is in our blood. Did I ever tell you that your great-grandmother was an opera singer?"

I wanted to laugh because I didn't remember mom telling me much of anything. "Opera? No shit?"

I'm not sure why but she started singing in this faux operatic voice. And it was loud. Embarrassingly loud.

"La donna è mobile,

Qual piuma al vento, Muta d'accento

E di pensierooooooo!"

She laughed as everyone stared at her and me. I wanted to crawl under the table.

Mom took a sip of coffee.

"Then there's your dad," she said, referring to the godfather of punk himself. She pointed to the Ramones pin on my leather jacket. "That's my girl!" She said.

It was weird hearing her refer to me as her girl.

"So what's with all the 80's metal posters?" I asked while we were on the topic of music.

She laughed and said, "Not taking any blame for that. That's all Jim's shit."

"Who's Jim?"

"I guess you could say he's my boyfriend. He's a goof and into some real shitty music."

"I guess so," I said.

"Believe me, I want to die every time he plays it or drags me to some metal fest concerts."

I wondered if Jim was as much of a jerkoff as I suspected.

Mom waved down the waitress for more coffee and said, "I've been thinking of doing this thing, this open mic at this bar downtown, but I think I'm too nervous."

"What's there to be nervous about?" I asked. In her day, mom toured everywhere, playing in front of large festival crowds. I didn't think a small open mic performance would have phased her in the slightest.

"You get rusty fast," she said adding more sugar to her coffee. "What if I can't sing anymore? What if I've lost my edge?"

Mom got silent and looked at me again in disbelief. "Jesus, I can't believe I'm sitting here with you. This is so fucked! But in a good way." She was smiling, so I smiled back, before staring into my half-filled coffee cup.

"You still have you-know-what?" She asked, cryptically changing the subject.

"What?"

"The guitar, dum-dum," she said, like I should have known what she meant. She was referring to my recently stolen guitar.

I shook my head.

"What?" She said, outraged.

"Stolen."

"Stolen?"

"Yup."

"It's gone?"

"Some guy ripped it off."

"Who?"

"Some loser who probably pawned it for drug money."

"He stole that beautiful fucking guitar? This is the Martin we're talking about?"

"Yeah, Mom, he stole that beautiful fucking guitar."

"Why?"

I wondered why she was so shocked over this. People do shitty things. It happens. She, of all people, should know this. Still, I offered an explanation that was a little over the line even for me: "Some people will do anything for a fix, right?"

She got quiet, rightly sensing this was meant to hurt her a little, but I think it hurt her a lot. Even as I sat there, I wondered why I suddenly shot so close to the jugular, just as we were kinda-sorta relating.

The waitress discretely left the bill, probably sensing the tension at our table. Mom picked it up and in a low hoarse voice said, "I should get back. Jim will be home soon and we're having people over. You're staying a while, I hope."

I shrugged, wondering if a while meant a couple of hours or a couple of days. She then got up. "I'll take care of this and use the bathroom. Go ahead and wait in the car."

Fifteen minutes later, I was still waiting. This is how it was with mom. Even as a kid, she always kept me waiting, always disappearing at the strangest times. Mom disappeared into bathrooms a lot and not because she had stomach issues. It was to get her fix. I figured this was why she sent me to the car this time, so I reclined the seat slightly, popped a Xan, and kept waiting. But as I started to doze, she suddenly busted out of the door, sprinting across the parking lot.

She jumped into my car and yelled, "Drive! Now! Just drive!"

Before I could ask what the hell was wrong, she screamed, "Go!" So I peeled out of the parking lot, nearly hitting a parked car in the process. Like a woman possessed, mom was breathing heavily and laughing as though on an adrenaline high. When we were a mile down the coastal road, I dared ask for an explanation, scared to death at what she might say.

Was she running from someone she owed money to? An old landlord? A dealer? When I finally asked, I braced myself, knowing anything was possible.

"What the hell was that, Mom?" I asked.

Suddenly, as calm as can be, she lit a cigarette and laughed again. "Don't worry about it," she said.

"Tell me!"

"It's fine," she said. "Don't worry about it."

Then it dawned on me. "You didn't pay the check, did you?"

She rolled down the window a few inches and blew out smoke, giggling. "What makes you say that?"

"Seems pretty obvious."

She shrugged. "The food sucks anyway, and I forgot my wallet. What do you want me to do?"

"I could've paid for it, Mom!" I said, remembering the cash I made from playing at the dock in Portland.

Mom puffed away and appeared far more chill than before. "Don't worry about it, I said. I'll pay them back later. I know the owner."

We drove around for another hour, not talking much, just sort of getting used to being in each other's orbit. I came close to telling her why I was there but didn't, wondering if it even mattered now considering she couldn't even pay for pancakes. It seemed not much had changed.

Trouble had a way of finding mom; or maybe she was good at finding trouble. Like me.

Whatever the case, it had been only an hour or so, and I was already driving her getaway car.

Chapter Seven

A low-riding yellow coupe with tinted windows was parked in the driveway when we returned to mom's trailer. I veered to the side of the road and parked. Neither of us moved, and mom looked like she had no intention of getting out right away. She seemed downbeat now. The thrill of screwing over the diner had faded.

"Uh, Mom, hello?" She was staring off into the woods.

She squinted over at me. My voice startled her.

"You're not moving."

"Give me a minute," she said, lighting up a cigarette.

I turned off the car and leaned back into the seat, unsure of what we were waiting for. "Is the heavy metal guy home?" I asked.

"Yup," she said, void of any enthusiasm.

"Will he care that I'm here?"

"He's a goof," she said separating her ponytail into two parts and tugging hard. "Who cares what he thinks?"

This was not reassuring.

With one hand gripping the door handle, she continued to stall for the next few minutes, like she was afraid to go into her own house. This gave me a really bad vibe. Then, all of a sudden, the trailer door flung open, and out came this odd looking guy in a black Kiss t-shirt tucked into gym pants. This had to be Jim, and at first glance, he irked me. His hair was long, greasy, and clearly dyed. But what bothered me most was his gross, creepy porn mustache.

The guy looked like a sidekick villain in a bad karate movie—the one who gets killed first. He seemed too preoccupied to notice us watching him drag a rusted metal ladder across their small lawn.

Mom glanced at me and grimaced. "Don't say it. I know. He's no Morrissey. I get it," she said as though she knew what I was thinking.

"No, he's definitely not," I said, giggling, noticing this guy had practically no chin.

"We can't all be young and cute forever. But just remember, you're sitting here because *I* screwed Joey Ramone."

"Lucky me," I said.

She caught my sarcasm and smirked. "How many girls get to call godfather of punk dad?"

"Most likely hundreds, the world over," I said.

Mom laughed. "Yeah, you're probably right." We watched porn-stache man mess around with the ladder and eventually start climbing it. "Jim's been futzing with this cable dish for days. It keeps breaking on us."

Jim was growing more frustrated by the second, swiping away a branch that kept getting in his way. His frustration soon resembled rage. At one point, he actually flicked off the dish. I asked myself, what sort of moron gives an inanimate object the finger?

I then noticed a car in the rear-view mirror coming upon us. It rolled slowly past and pulled into mom's driveway. A short, round guy with a backward baseball cap stepped out and, Jim, after noticing, scurried down the ladder.

"Are you expecting company?" I asked.

"Shit," mom whispered to herself.

"What?" I asked, sensing trouble.

"Jim is not happy with this goofball."

After exchanging words, Jim shoved the guy against his car. Jim, who was much smaller, somehow managed to pin the bigger guy against his own vehicle. The guy nodded repeatedly as Jim yelled in his face before letting him go back to his car. As the guy drove off, Jim kicked the side of his car and then stormed back into the trailer.

"What the hell just happened?" I asked.

"Who knows?" Mom said, like this was a somewhat normal occurrence.

"Did you know that guy?"

"I'm not sure it's a good time," mom said.

"So what are you saying?"

Mom sunk back into the car seat. "I don't know. Fuck my life!" She looked frustrated, nervous, and was clawing at her arms again.

Mom, I gathered, was afraid or embarrassed—probably both—to introduce me to this Jim loser. I had the feeling I was probably one of the last people he wanted to know. Now I really didn't want to be there. "Whatever. I should go," I said, convinced my visit was a dumb idea.

"No!" she sat right up. "Just stay here a minute. I'll tell him you're here and that you're spending the night. Case closed."

"No, it's okay."

"Yes!"

"I can't spend the night."

"Why not?"

I stammered. I couldn't give a real reason other than I didn't want to. It just felt weird. "Don't be like that," she said. "You came all the way up here. You *have* to stay."

I didn't argue. "What about *him*?" I gestured toward Jim who was outside again, heading back up the ladder.

"Jim can get pissy, but so what? Just ignore him. You just got here."

Without even meeting the guy, I could already tell that Jim was exactly the kind of jerkoff you'd expect mom to be with. Their relationship *had* to be messed up. With mom, there was always more to the story, always something she wasn't telling you.

"I know you probably want to get out of here," she said wiping a bit of pancake of the side of my chin, "but I haven't seen you in forever. It wouldn't hurt to stay a bit, would it?"

I gave her an angsty shrug. "I guess not."

She patted my hand. "Give me a sec," she said as she got out of the car and sashayed over to Jim who seemed on the verge of ripping the dish off the tree. They exchanged a few words, then Jim glared over at me with the biggest *are you f-ing serious?* expression I'd ever seen. We made eye contact for a split second, but I turned away, clenching the pills in my jacket pocket. With a screwdriver in his mouth, he came down the ladder, not looking the lightest bit thrilled.

I wanted to peel out and drive away, but instead, I froze as mom waved me over with her cigarette hand. I stepped out of the car and ambled over. Jim, with hands on hips, never took his eyes off me.

Mom looked nervous as hell as she introduced us. "This is Sheena."

Jim did not offer a handshake, a smile, or even a nod. "So this is your kid?" He said, like I wasn't standing there in front of him.

Mom let out a nervous laugh. "She's not a kid no more. This girl here is a high school grad now. Can you believe it? Me, I got a kid with a high school diploma."

Jim focused on me with these icy, vacant eyes. I was creeped out. It was like he was sizing me up, like he was suspicious of me.

"You need to crash?" He said.

By his tone, I could tell this was the last thing he wanted. "Not really. It's okay," I said, wanting nothing more than to leave.

"Stop it," mom insisted placing her hand on my shoulder. "You're staying."

"It's fine…" I really didn't know what to say. I was mad at myself for even being there, without really thinking it all through. After a little more coaxing from mom, I gave in.

"But you'll have to put up with some of his goofy friends," she said. "They'll be over later apparently."

"You like ultimate cage fighting?" He asked.

"Not really," I said.

He grunted like it was the wrong answer and started back up the ladder.

I couldn't have felt less welcome, and the last thing I wanted was to spend the night in a trailer with this guy, especially with his friends there. I didn't get it. What did mom see in him? Even at her age, mom could've done a lot better.

Mom watched Jim continue to struggle with the dish. "I feel I should warn you," she said. "Jim's friends…they're a little wild."

"Wild how?"

"Let's just say that they like a party. Especially when there's a fight on."

Mom then went inside and took forever to use the bathroom. When she came back, something was different about her. She looked dazed. I knew she was high, or should I say higher than she already was. She brought me around the trailer, down through a small wooded path that led into a clearing next to a running stream. We sat in two lawn chairs next to a burned-out campfire filled with broken beer bottles and cigarette butts.

"This is my spot. No one else's," she said, slurring every word. It wasn't a Zen garden or anything, but I could see why she liked it. The sound of the water was nice and the trees in full bloom made it a nice hiding spot.

Mom lit another cigarette. "I come down here with my guitar sometimes. To get away from all the shit."

"Is there a lot of shit?"

"There's always a lot of shit," she said, watching the restless water.

I noticed mom's eyes growing heavier by the second; but I knew it wasn't because she was tired. It was because she was high. Really high. But just when I thought she was out cold, mom perked up when a dog in a nearby yard barked or if a car passed. This happened a few times, then she started muttering incoherently. I wasn't sure if she was talking to me or to herself in some drug-induced dream.

After a minute or two, I heard her say something reasonably audible. It almost sounded like, "I didn't want to leave," but I wasn't quite sure. And if she really said this, how could I really believe it? If mom really wanted me, I mean *really, really* wanted me, wouldn't she have found a way? Wouldn't she have done everything to overcome her shit?

Even if I wanted to ask her these questions, she wouldn't have heard me.

She was asleep.

But in my mind, like so many times before, I still spoke to her, I screamed at her, I hugged her close. As I watched her drift in and out of her drug-fog, I suddenly felt dumb being there, dumb for expecting something. But the more I thought about it, sitting in that lawn chair, should I *really* be pissed at her? When it comes down to it, my existence came down to some horny rock star deciding to screw some random groupie.

I wasn't born from any real motherly desire; there was no love there. She never asked for me. Why did I ever expect anything from her? Why did I expect anything now?

As usual, this kind of impossible thinking gave me a headache, so I popped a Xan and soon entered a fog of my own. I lost count of how many were in me, but it was enough to make my eyes heavy.

As the stream soothed me, I allowed myself to drift off to sleep in a shaky lawn chair on the edge of a trailer park, next to my mom for the first time in who knows when; and for the first time in a long time, I was close to her.

Chapter Eight

A couple of hours later, just as it was getting dark, Jim kicked our chairs and announced his friends would be arriving 'Any fuckin' minute', and so we dragged ourselves back to the trailer, per Jim's order, and started to clean. I washed a mountain of dishes piled in the sink while mom vacuumed and Jim futzed behind the TV trying to get a signal from the dish. A pizza guy soon arrived followed by six of Jim's friends not long after, all of them toting beer, wearing sweatpants and backward caps, passing me with creepy grins in my direction. They were exactly how I imagined Jim's friends would be.

When Jim finally found a signal, everyone cracked open beers and planted themselves in front of the TV, making dumb jokes that were mostly dirty. They grew more obnoxious by the minute, yelling at the screen, and getting off on every punch and kick. Other than the occasional perverted stares, I was mostly ignored, that is until one guy wearing a black hoodie and dark framed glasses zeroed in on me.

"Hey, Vonny, so this is your daughter, huh?" He asked with a mouthful of pizza.

"You're not gonna introduce me?" It was like I wasn't there until now. And mom wasn't even paying attention; she was at the kitchen table, looking miserable, scribbling away in a notebook, taking the occasional swig from a bottle of clear liquid.

"It's a good thing she doesn't know you," she said without looking up. "Let's keep it that way."

The guy laughed, thinking mom was making a joke, but I knew she wasn't joking.

He kept staring. "I'm Mike," he said.

I wanted to say, 'So what?' but I just shrugged, which pretty much meant the same thing. "So you ain't gonna tell me *your* name?" He said, laughing, taking a mammoth gulp of beer.

I shook my head.

He laughed. "The apple doesn't fall far, does it, Von?"

"Let's hope it does," mom said before taking another drink.

The guy kept taking his eyes off the TV and smiling at me like it was his intention to creep me out. And believe me, he succeeded. In an attempt to ignore him, I played Tetris on my phone, all the while theorizing about what mom was writing on that pad. Was she doodling out of sheer boredom, making a shopping list, or was it something more meaningful, something creative? I wanted to think she was writing song lyrics or poetry. This would have meant a spark was still there, that something within her was still reaching toward beauty.

As this horrible night wore on, I took the occasional stroll down the dirt shore road, passing other trailers, many filled with parties of their own. At one point, I nearly got in my car and drove off, but for some reason, I just couldn't bring myself to do it. I kept going back to the trailer, and each time, everyone looked higher and drunker. Now and then, mom would disappear into the bedroom and return with an even more glazed look in her eyes.

I didn't physically see any drugs but I knew they were there, hidden somewhere. If I wasn't around, it would have been all out in the open— needles, bags of powder, maybe lines of coke on the coffee table. Hiding it seemed like such a charade, but mom, I imagined, made sure I didn't see what was obviously going on.

It was around midnight when I returned from my last walk. Jim and a couple of others were still glued to the TV while the other two guys were passed out in chairs. But I didn't see mom anywhere. Doing my best to go unnoticed, I passed her bedroom and peeked into the partially open door; and there she was, practically comatose, on top of the covers and still in her clothes. There was no way of knowing how high she was by now, but I was sure she was out for the night.

Nervous that she was going to fall out of bed and break her neck, I tiptoed into the room and pulled her fully onto the bed and covered her. She never once opened her eyes. As I made my way back out, I nearly kicked over a guitar leaned up against the foot of the bed, and it might have been the most revolting guitar I'd ever seen. It was an acoustic guitar decorated with airbrushed skulls, purple lightning bolts, flames, and several signatures which I assumed belonged to some washed up metal rockers from the 80s.

It couldn't have been mom's guitar. I picked it up by the neck and noticed it was far heavier than any acoustic should be. I then noticed the sound hole below the strings was stuffed with small bags filled with white powder. I was stunned. That hideous guitar was a hiding place for mom's medicine, but it was crammed with enough white powder for twenty addicts. This is when it became obvious that Jim—perhaps mom, too—was dealing.

Disgusted, I leaned the guitar against the bed and left the room without a sound, hoping no one noticed me. Then, as I helped myself to a glass of water, I realized mom left her notebook open on the table. Thinking no one would care, I sat down and read, and just as I'd hoped, it was a book of poetry, perhaps lyrics, all written in a barely legible scrawl. A lot of it made no sense, but some of it expressed pain. One line stood out:

I don't know how to feel. What is real? What is real?

After pursuing for a few minutes, I slid the notebook back in the exact same position. I then noticed my name written in the margins but with a heart drawn around it. This made me feel amazing. But when I looked up, Jim was eying me like he caught me in some horrible act. I looked away, but in my head, I told him to go to hell. To fuck off. After a swig of beer, he went back to watching TV.

What am I doing here? I asked myself. Most kids on graduation night were out partying with friends, at real parties, drinking, dancing, feeling a lust for life. Yet there I was, in a dumpy trailer with a bunch of oafs and my drugged-out mother passed out in the next room. All this to get money for school. My guess was that the money was gone.

Maybe it was because I was so depressed, but as soon as I noticed mom's liquor was still on the table, I pulled it close and took a swing. It burned like hell but I took another, and then another, not caring if it burned like hell, as long as it numbed me. Soon, after putting the bottle down, I lowered my head onto the table and fell asleep on mom's notebook.

Hours later, I woke up confused to find myself on the floor under the table with zero memory of how I got down there. Groggy as hell, with my head pounding, it took me a minute to realize someone was close by—so close I could smell him and hear his breath. I lifted my head and saw it was the creep in the black hoodie. Before I could react, he grabbed my ass and in a beastly moan said, "Party's not over, is it?" I sat up and banged my head hard on the bottom of the table.

"What the fuck?" I yelled, butchering my throat.

He pulled me closer. "Sshh. What's your deal? Calm the hell down."

Without hesitating, I punched the asshole square in the face before leaping to my feet. As he pulled away holding his face, I knew that I hit him square in the nose. Jim woke and jumped out of his recliner as the two other idiot friends stirred on the couch. I sprinted out of the trailer toward my car but realized I forgot my key, so I stormed back in and yanked it off the kitchen chair, knocking it over in the process. Jim was already in the bedroom screaming at mom.

"You didn't tell me she's a little psycho!" He screamed. "Mike's goddamn nose is bleeding everywhere!"

Mom was awake but didn't sound totally with it. "I'm sure he asked for it. Who doesn't want to punch Mike?"

Mike had blood-soaked paper towels bunched up against his nose. "Crazy bitch," he kept saying.

"Crazy, why?" I screamed. "Because I wouldn't let you go down my pants?"

"She's full of shit," he kept saying.

"You're a fucking creep!" I yelled.

Mom rubbed her eyes and looked only half there. "Can you guys just get out? Leave."

Jim's friends sat there until mom finally exploded. "Get the hell out!" They stood up at once and left immediately.

This pissed Jim off big time. "What the hell does she want from you, anyway?" Jim spotted me and said, "What do you want? I mean, who *are* you?"

I stormed out the door and across the lawn, this time with my bag and my keys. Jim may have been right to suspect me of being there for other unsaid reasons, but there was no way I was going to make any demands from mom with him around. Mom called my name as the screen door slammed behind me but I ignored it. I then heard screaming, chairs being kicked around, doors slamming. Still, I didn't turn around, but I knew what was going on.

I always knew when terrible shit was going down, and if anyone in the other trailers cared to listen, if things were actually fair, the cops would show up and arrest Jim for what I feared he was doing to mom.

Why didn't I turn around and go back in? Why didn't I do anything to help? There's no good reason. There's not even a bad reason. *Who was I?* It was actually a good question, and I didn't really have an answer. As I drove off into the night, I didn't feel much more than a scared little girl.

Chapter Nine

Even though I never went back into the trailer that night, I was afraid to go too far, afraid to leave mom alone with that asshole. So I slept in the car, waking up every half hour or so, looking into the trailer which was now quiet and still. With mom's world more messed up than I imagined, the idea of getting money from her seemed so distant and silly now. She lived in a world I was always determined to run from, yet there I was, still there.

But why? What was keeping me from driving back home and forgetting I ever made the trip in the first place? Around noon, mom came out of the trailer for her morning smoke and caught me sitting in my car. She smiled and waved but went back inside. After a minute or so, she came back out and waved me over. She immediately apologized for last night's horror show and insisted I let Jim apologize too, so I followed her in and saw the jerk face pouring coffee in the kitchen pantry.

"About last night," he grumbled, not looking up at me. "I was completely shit-faced. Couldn't even tell you what happened if you held a gun to my head. But I guess I was a bit rude. It is what it is." It was obvious a lame apology—if you want to call it an apology—was mom's idea, not his, and it was the exact kind you'd expect from him. Even if his apology was real, I wouldn't have accepted it anyhow, never mind one that blamed his asshole behavior on alcohol.

"This goofball can't drink," mom reiterated.

I stared at the floor, unable to even look at Jim. I could barely look at mom for putting up with this ogre and for making excuses for him. Their world seemed so toxic, and it was obvious he did not love her but held some Svengali-like power over her life. Mom looked so helpless, drained of life as she stood there. Like a zombie. And I was mad at myself, asking how I could sit in my car all night and not call the police or run back into the house to help mom.

Mom and I spent most of that morning sitting around by the stream, not talking much, but I had the feeling we were both wondering what *this* was. Were we making a go at something like a relationship? A friendship, or something? Or was this just a long hello? As the morning wore on, though, it was clear that mom, who was dozing off in her chair, was not thinking much of anything. At one point, as she slept, I went back to the trailer to pee, passing her room.

I glanced in and saw Jim reaching into the skull guitar, and at the risk of him seeing me, I watched as he pulled out a small bag of mom's medicine. I dashed out of the trailer without using the bathroom. A car pulled up not long after and. Jim got in. After a brief exchange with whoever it was, he got out and the car drove off. I knew I had to be witnessing a drug deal.

The sound of the car woke mom, and after a couple of minutes of silence, I just had to say something, so I blurted out, "What's up with that guitar?"

"What guitar?"

"The ugly one with the skulls and lightning bolts?"

"How do you know about that?" She asked, clearly stunned.

"You disappeared and I was worried. So I looked in your room. It was on your bed." Mom got quiet. She was wondering what I knew. I could read it on her face.

Then she smiled. "You were checking on me? You're too cute," she said. "Don't worry about that."

"Is it yours?"

"It's Jim's. He paid a lot of money for that. Motley Cru signed it at a backstage meet and greet. You have no idea how much he loves that thing."

"I'll bet he does," I said.

"I hate it. I hate that guitar."

I'm not sure why but I didn't press her to explain what it contained. What difference would it make? She had to suspect I knew something.

Later on, I went to a nearby pharmacy to pick up a toothbrush, deodorant, and a few snacks. When I came back, I could hear mom and Jim screaming at each other again before I even opened the car door. I got out and crossed the road, amazed at how little they cared about anyone hearing them in the other trailers. I guessed it was a regular thing.

I stayed outside around the yard, occasionally wandering back down to the brook, swearing that if Jim laid one finger on mom, I'd punch his face and call the cops. Whenever I got close to the trailer, I heard they were mostly fighting over me being there. Jim kept saying I was in the way.

"She's my daughter!" Mom kept yelling. "What do you want me to do?"

And it didn't take long for me to suspect what Jim meant by *in the way*. The drug deals happened every hour or so; I knew exactly what was going on. But it was even harder to see my own mother hurrying the deliveries out to the cars.

Later that afternoon, after the fighting died down, Jim jumped into his car and drove off somewhere. Not seeing any sign of mom, I went back in the trailer and ran to her bedroom door and heard nothing inside but the sound of a window fan. Gently, I pushed open the door and saw her lying there, on her stomach again, not moving at all. This freaked me out, so I ran over.

"Mom!" I said, shaking her. She didn't wake up, but with one hand flat on her back, I was relieved to hear her breathing. Her shirt was drenched with sweat, strings of her hair were hanging off the bed. The way she'd snort and gasp for air, I knew it was something more than an afternoon nap, and when I saw what was on the nightstand, I knew exactly what was going on.

I'd seen one before.

A fucking needle.

I wrapped a wet strand of hair behind her ear, so I could see her eyes. They were half open.

I shook her gently. "Mom?"

She blinked and fixed her gaze on me, not fully aware of where she was or who was talking to her. She turned and faced the wall.

This was not shocking; from a very young age, I knew this is what my mother did, what she lived for. So why did it hurt to see her like this now? I stayed there on the bed, waiting for her to come down from her high. She barely moved, and the occasional moan and gasp for air kept me on edge the entire time. After an hour, I heard Jim come home and toss his keys onto the table. He bulldozed the bedroom door and actually started laughing when he saw me sitting there on the bed. I almost punched him.

"And you thought she'd be baking you cookies by now?" He said, laughing his ass off.

"You think this is funny?" My voice wasn't loud, but it cracked with a blend of sadness and rage.

"Come on, lighten up…" he said, looking over at the needle and then at me. His laughter trailed off. "Don't tell me you're surprised by this. Thought she was gonna change?"

I gave him my best go-to-hell glare. "What I think is none of your business," was all I could think to say, and I don't think he liked it one bit.

"Hell yeah, it's my business," he said. He shook his head, opened the closet, and took out his skull guitar case. He opened it up on the floor, pocketed a couple of bags—not caring what I saw—then closed it.

"Not sure what you came here for out of nowhere," he said, "but you're wasting your time with her." He gestured toward mom like she was some sort of non-entity then left the room. But I didn't. I sat with her for more than two hours, watching her breathe, making sure she was facing up.

Finally, she stirred in her bed like she was waking from a nightmare, then slowly, she opened her eyes and propelled herself up. After rubbing her face for a while, mom noticed I was there.

"Sheena?" She said.

"I'm here," I said.

She looked over at the needle and then at me. "I'm a piece of shit," she said in a whisper.

I wasn't sure if she wanted me to argue with her about this, but I didn't. She reached over and sipped her water bottle. I knew she was thinking about what to say next, like she wanted to give some kind of explanation. But there was nothing to say. There was no hiding from it now, no lie she could tell me, no excuse she could make. It was out in the open, and I wasn't a little girl anymore.

"I need you to know that I hate doing this," she said. "I don't want to do this."

"Then why do you?" I asked.

Mom paused like she was really trying to come up with the best answer. But all she said was, "I don't know."

"Stop then," I said, knowing it was dumb.

"You don't just stop," she said, not really answering the question. "It's real fucking hard."

"Do you want to stop?"

She didn't answer me; instead, she swiped her needle off the nightstand onto the floor and sat up more. "Can you stay around?" She asked. "Please? Stay with me."

I wasn't sure why she wanted me there. Why now? What purpose did I serve? Whatever the reason, I decided to hang around; it's not like I had anywhere else to go. But after one day, I got so anxious and bored that I started cleaning the trailer. I just had to do something. It began with doing the dishes, then sweeping, then scrubbing the counters. Mom, inspired to join in, started organizing her closets; we even made several trips to the local landfill to get rid of some of her clutter.

We even did some yard work—bagging leaves, mowing, raking. Mom did her best but was weak and horribly out of shape, constantly taking smoke breaks. She often went inside to lie down on the couch. By keeping busy, I found myself popping fewer Xans but still noticed my supply was dangerously low. This was only supposed to be a quick visit.

After a few days of this, mom turned to me as we were bagging leaves and said, out of nowhere, "Seventy-two hours."

I looked at her, confusedly. "Seventy-two hours what?"

"Sober." Like a little kid, she smiled proudly.

It took me a minute, and I probably should've sounded happier and more impressed, but all I said was, "That's cool, Mom." Maybe I wasn't bowled over because I couldn't bring myself to fully believe her.

But I was slightly more convinced the next afternoon as she practiced for the open mic she had mentioned at the diner. We were sitting by the brook as I watched her struggle to even strum the guitar. Her hands were shaking; she could barely hold onto the pick. It was hard to imagine she was ever in a band that was signed to a record deal. And it had to be more than nerves. She was withdrawing like crazy.

"This gig's got me really stressed to pieces," she said. "Don't know why I even signed up."

"What songs will you play?" I asked.

Mom put her head on the guitar. "No fuckin' idea. Any suggestions?"

I didn't know what to tell her. Mom's playing was hopeless and so not ready to perform. Then, out of nowhere, she started singing. She was a little flat but it wasn't totally horrible. The melody was pretty but her slurring made it difficult to understand the words.

"What song is that?" I asked once she finished.

"Nothing really. Just some goofy thing I came up with."

"You wrote that?" I asked.

She looked down at her guitar. "It's so hard to come up with new stuff at my age. It's like a spirit leaves you at some point. I don't know how to explain it." I knew what she meant.

"Let's get the hell out of here," she said suddenly.

"Where?" I asked.

"Anywhere but here," she said, already on her feet. It seems she had enough.

I followed her into the trailer. She pulled out a roll of cash from a pair of Jim's jeans that were draped over a chair. She looked up like she forgot I was there.

"You didn't see that," she said.

"See what?" I replied with a smile.

"I know exactly where we'll go!" She said in a surge of inspiration. I chased to my car. She had the coordination of a drunk newborn giraffe, always about to trip or bump into something. All these manic adrenaline rushes seemed to come out of nowhere. This whole time I kept thinking that her life was worse than I had imagined. Turns out she had a suspended license—according to the Trenton Facebook page of shame—so I couldn't imagine her leaving the house much or doing much more than getting high.

"I gotta take you to this killer music store downtown," she said as we drove off. "You like vinyl?"

"Records?" I asked.

"Yeah, you know those black shiny disks that spin around on a turntable?"

"I know what vinyl records are, Mom! What's the big deal?"

"If you never heard shit on vinyl, you've never heard shit," she said.

We got in the car and I followed mom's directions into the center of town which was like something you'd see in a Norman Rockwell calendar. After we parked, mom dragged me by the arm into this shop called Mainely Music. The store was stocked from floor to ceiling with stacks of old records, the walls were papered with old promo posters of classic albums, some I recognized, like *Abbey Road* and *The Wall.* Mom was in heaven, rummaging through the bins and chatting with the owner whom she seemed to know well.

"Your mom was a force of nature," he said to me, pulling a record out of a crate. With his graying beard, bandanna, and Rolling Stones t-shirt, the guy looked like a true professor of rock and roll.

"I bet she was," I said.

"Look!" The old guy came over and showed a copy of mom's only album from when she was in her band, Slug Sex. The album was called *Paper Moon*, which I thought was a killer title.

The cover art was some abstract painting of a moon face.

"Your mom was an incredible live performer," he said. "She controlled the room."

"I still am," mom protested.

"Oh, yeah? When will you start gigging again?" The owner seemed genuinely interested but also surprised.

"I'm thinking about it," she said. That open mic idea was one thing, but I couldn't imagine mom was in any shape for real live performance. Not without embarrassing herself.

"Wait! You gotta see this, if I can find it." The old guy told me to hold on as he went to the other end of the store and dug through a couple of boxes. After a minute, he pulled out an old VHS tape and held it up proudly.

"Found it!" He said. "You two are gonna shit when you see this."

"What do you have now?" Mom asked.

"An antique," he said.

"Slug Sex?" I asked as my face lit up.

"Live!" He said.

We followed him to another corner of the store where a TV older than me was looping 80's music videos. He ejected that tape, blew dust off the one he found and shoved it into the VCR.

"You gotta see this, kid," he said, grinning at me like he was about to reveal a secret. At first, the image was scrambled, but after he messed with the buttons, I saw it was raw concert footage. The audio was just as low-fi but I recognized mom's voice cutting through the distortion. I recognized her yelling anywhere.

"*That* is your mother on *that* stage," the store owner said.

"Turn that shit off!" Mom said, blushing.

He ignored her demand, so I watched for at least fifteen minutes while mom shopped, occasionally shouting at me to 'Burn the tape!'. But I was fascinated by it. It was mind-blowing that the crazy girl on that stage was mom; it was weird seeing her so full of life. She controlled that room, strumming her guitar with all the ferocity of Patti Smith in her prime. Her voice soared over the rest of the band, over the screams from the riotous audience. She was a girl possessed.

Mom then did one of the coolest things I ever saw on tape.

As the band ended a song, she smashed the hell out of her guitar in two swings, destroying the fuck out of it against an amp. Pieces went into the crowd that was screaming for more.

The store owner noticed how impressed I was.

"She was a killer," he said. "Ain't that right, Vonnie?"

Mom didn't seem interested. "Ancient history," she said, sauntering over, carrying a record. "I'm definitely getting you this! It'll be your first vinyl record!" She handed it to me like it was sacred. The cover had a banana on it. "You know the Velvet Underground, right?"

"Kinda, yeah," I said.

She took back the record. "You'll like this one. It started everything."

"Thanks, but I don't have a record player."

"Shit, right," she said.

The owner went to the stockroom and came back with something that looked more like a suitcase. "Check this out," he said. "It's a relic but it's really damn cool. Battery operated." He opened it and revealed a turntable. He put on the Velvet Underground record and lowered the needle, then out of the side speaker came the sneering croon of Lou Reed.

The first track was a slow tune called *Sunday Morning*, which I later learned is a song about paranoia. Mom said the second song, *Waiting For My Man*, was the first punk song ever…the 'Big Bang'. And as the rest of the first side was unleashed from that little suitcase, as it nearly blew those tiny speakers, mom scurried from one crate to the next, gathering records she said I just had to have. When she was finished, she was barely able to lift them onto the counter.

"This is the greatest stack of records ever assembled," she declared. "The holy canon."

This was the happiest I'd seen her since arriving in Maine, which meant it may have been the happiest I had ever seen her. The owner entered everything into an old register, adding up the two dozen or so albums, plus the record player.

"I'll go ahead and knock off $25 simply because it's you," he said, "and because it's for educational purposes. Let's call it an even $250."

Mom pulled out the cash she probably wasn't supposed to have and peeled off three one hundred dollar bills.

"You really don't have to, Mom," I protested.

"Sure I do!" She said. "I want to."

We left the shop lugging the records and the suitcase record player and made our way down the street. Mom looked proud of herself as we placed it all in the trunk of my car. As we drove off, she told me her plan.

"Here's the deal," she said. "It's my duty as your mother to educate you about each of those records. We'll listen to one a day and I'll tell you why it's fucking great."

I knew this was her way of trying, so I decided to indulge her. "Alright…cool," I said.

"You won't be taught this stuff in college," she said.

"There's like thirty records there, Mom," I said. "How long do you think I'm staying?"

She didn't answer right away. She thought about it and said, "Maybe for a little while longer?"

It was kind of nice that she wanted me there. But I couldn't imagine hanging around for *too* much longer. Not with porn-stache around.

"Jim won't be into that idea," I said.

"Fuck him," she said. "It's my place too. You're my daughter so he'll have to deal, right?"

I wasn't really sure where mom was going with this. She was in the grip of severe heroin addiction; why did she suddenly want me around. Sure, it did feel good to be wanted, but was this only on the whim of a junky? Was I some kind of novelty for her? Was she playing mommy because it felt good at the moment? What about the next day? What about the next time she had to choose me over the needle? I wanted to ask her but didn't really know how.

"What happens when we run out of records?" I asked instead.

"We can always get more," she said.

Later on, we took a long drive through narrow back roads to some state park where we parked in a small lot next to a few hiking trails. There, we took the turntable out of the trunk and fired it up so we could listen to the other side of the Velvet Underground and Nico record. The young families having lunch on nearby picnic tables had no idea what to make of these two weirdos playing old weirdo music, disturbing the peace, and not giving a shit.

Halfway through side two, mom ran back to the car, got out her guitar, and started to play along with the record, sometimes moving the needle back so she could get the chords right. She paid special attention to what she played during a song called *I'll Be Your Mirror* which, two measures in, struck me as beautiful.

"I was thinking about doing this one," she said, "for the open mic. What do you think?" I told her it was a great choice.

She quickly found the chords and, after the second time through, sang along. Mom's was a smoker's voice, for sure, but she still had excellent pitch and some dark, tender nuance—a deep, eccentric voice with plenty of soul. After a third time, she turned off the record player and sang it alone. It was a beautiful and heartbreaking take on the song. Even the families at the picnic table listened. I was impressed and almost told her so.

On our way back to her trailer, along the coastal road, we passed this dingy rest stop where I saw a familiar vehicle parked—a truck with a camper in the back, one that could only belong to one asshole. Doubting my own eyes, I spun my head around and gasped, nearly swerving off the road.

"What the hell?" Mom hollered, bracing herself with both hands on the dashboard.

"It's so him!" I said as it fully sunk in. It was definitely him. I slammed on the breaks and did a very illegal U-turn.

"It's who?" Mom asked, hanging on to her seat.

"That guy!"

"What guy?"

"The guy who ripped off my guitar! His truck is at that rest stop!"

Mom sat up. "Show me," she demanded.

I pulled out my phone as we approached the rest stop.

"What are you doing?" She asked.

"Calling the cops," I said, pulling in.

She grabbed my phone. "Screw that. Just park."

"Mom…"

"Listen to your mother. Just park. We don't need the cops."

Reluctantly, I did what she said and parked a safe distance away. I wasn't exactly sure how mom wanted to handle this, but I was sure a confrontation was inevitable, so we sat and waited. I could tell mom was really pissed off as she kept wringing her hands.

"What are you going to do?" I asked her, running my fingers through my hair. "Mom?" Before she answered, the door to the truck opened. "Oh my god—he's coming out!" I said. "Just let me call the police." I nabbed my phone off her, and again mom snapped it out of my fingers.

"No!" She said. "You're sure that's him?"

"Yeah, that's Tim or whatever his name is," I said, as he crossed the parking lot, wearing the same t-shirt and jeans he was wearing in Portland. He stopped in front of the restroom door and read a sign that was posted. After tugging on the door handle in vain, he went into a nearby porta-potty.

Mom smiled and said, "Don't move and keep the car running."

"What are you doing, Mom?" I tried to hold her arm but she slipped out of the car with this evil grin. I called for her but she ran toward the truck, ignoring me entirely. My heart was racing as I could do nothing but watch as she kept going until she got there. Without a second of hesitation, she opened the unlocked trailer door, looked over to me, giving me a thumbs up.

My anxiety spun out of control when she crawled inside. The only thing I could do was watch, completely frozen, helpless.

Thirty seconds passed like thirty minutes, and there was still no sign of her. I kept looking over, expecting him to catch her in the act; and when I couldn't stand it any longer, mom came out with my guitar case, giving me a thumbs up again. I placed my foot lightly on the gas, but instead of running back to the car, she strutted over to the porta-potty, grinning, like she had zero fear of getting caught.

I shouted, "Mom! What are you doing?" but she totally ignored me, put down the guitar case and started to push the side of the porta-potty. I wanted to run out and stop her but was too numb to actually move.

I shouted at her again: "Mom! Cut the shit, let's go!" And again, she ignored me. She was really trying, putting all her strength into it, turning bright red. After two or three rocks, it almost went over. Giving in, I jumped out and helped her push until the thing fell right the fuck over. Laughing, mom scooped up the guitar and we sprinted back to my car, almost falling over each other, cracking up.

My tires screeched as we took off; I stared in my rear-view mirror and actually saw him crawling out of the vault of shit. I was horrified but a deep sense of joy overcame me when I saw his expression—an expression that could only come from being covered in human filth. Part of me wished he had seen me, and maybe he had his suspicions when he realized the guitar was gone. Maybe it was a karmic lesson that sometimes the universe has to put its foot down.

I was the getaway driver once again but I didn't mind it so much this time. For the first mile, we pretty much laughed non-stop. All this insanity reminded me of the stories of how crazy mom was in her day, like the time she supposedly ran on stage during a Beastie Boys show and flashed the crowd, and got kicked out of the venue. And then when her band was recording her first album, rumor has it she brought her dead parrot into the studio and told the engineer to mic it up.

Apparently, she wanted to record its 'transitioning aura' and actually demanded several takes. I guess that was mom, and age did not seem to mellow her out all that much after all.

Honestly, this was the side of her I had hoped to see. But it wasn't long before I started to again see the parts I didn't like.

The next couple of days were far less eventful. Mom wasn't feeling well, so I hung around the house most of the time and nursed her. She'd disappear into her bedroom to 'nap', so I'd kill time by taking long walks and playing my guitar by the brook while trying to avoid Jim who was always coming and going and always pissy as hell.

And then it happened, at an arcade of all places, another place I just *had* to see, a place called Fun Town which was something right out of an 80's movie—two floors of old arcade games. We were having a blast playing Ski-Ball, Pacman, and air hockey. We laughed, won tickets, and gave each other high-fives. It was something I could really get used to—the whole mother-daughter thing, but I kept pulling back from believing it was an actual possibility, like it could really happen.

Just when I started to think too much about it, I shrugged it off, like you do when you fantasize about something too good to be true—like winning the lottery. But I knew something was wrong once she kept disappearing into the bathroom, for sometimes up to twenty minutes. She'd come out sweaty, pale, out of breath, looking like she was about to collapse. When I asked her what was wrong, she'd brushed it off and pretend she was okay, but I knew she wasn't.

She was in hell. Everything about her was restless. She looked paranoid, her weak frame trembled as she wandered from game to game, pretending to have fun.

"What's going on, Mom?" I asked her as she tried to play pinball. "Tell me." She knew I knew the truth but she tried to cover it up anyhow.

"I keep getting these migraines," she said. "Let me throw some cold water on my face. I'll be okay."

Again, she disappeared into the bathroom for what seemed like the twentieth time. I sat around and waited by a row of pinball machines.

That chick's a live wire, ain't she?

I turned toward that deep familiar voice and saw dad lighting up some old UFO pinball machine.

"What the hell am I doing here?" I asked him.

That's up to you, he said.

"That doesn't help, Dad."

You came for money, right? Well?

"Well, what?"

Did you get any?

"No."

Why not?

"I don't know. Haven't asked."

What are you waiting for?

I really didn't know what to tell him. I didn't even have an answer for myself. "There's more to this than I thought," I said biting down on my lower lip. "There's a lot more."

Like what?

I stared at the bathroom door, watching for mom to come out. "Mom's suffering." Dad turned from his game and leaned against the machine. The pinball lights were reflecting in his glasses as he looked at me.

Withdrawal is no joke. But your mother is a survivor. So are you.

"How would you know?" I asked.

You think she was just another chick to me, don't you?

"She wasn't?"

Your mom was a cool shit. I saw her band a couple times here and there. I remember the night you happened. We got tacos at this great hole-in-the-wall in Brooklyn, we listened to some New York Dolls records at my apartment. Talked all night about music.

"Then you ditched her. And me."

Dad turned back to his game and shot another ball up the slot. *We had a tour in Japan, kiddo. Wasn't in the cards.*

"Did you even know about me?" I asked him.

He let the silver ball roll down between the paddles. *That doesn't matter. I know about you now, right?*

"Do you really?" I asked.

Dad ignored the question and asked a question of his own. *Who's gonna be there for her if not you?*

"What do you mean?" When I looked over for an explanation, he was gone.

By now, mom had been in that bathroom for twenty-five minutes. I wanted to see through the door. But then again, I didn't need to. I could almost see her vomiting in the toilet, then getting up and looking in the mirror, examining her own frightened eyes, scratching her torn-up arms. I saw her sitting on the toilet, holding her head, praying for the strength to march back out and pretend she wasn't in hell. And once she did, was I going to pretend along with her?

When she came out, her first words were, "Take me home, Sheena."

I saw the sweat and pain oozing out of her pores. It felt like she wanted to be with me but she wanted to be with her needle more. But the last place I thought she should be was back at her trailer, where it was easy to feed the demon inside her.

"Don't make me bring you back there," I said as I tagged after her toward the exit.

It wasn't like she was ignoring me on purpose. It's just that anything I said couldn't have mattered to her at that moment. There was only one thing on her mind.

I dragged myself behind her as she rushed through the parking lot, paying little mind to the moving cars. I trailed closely, thinking of ways to plead with her, to keep her from going back to that trailer. She was running now.

"Mom! Can you just hold on one minute?" I said.

She stopped and glared at me. "What the fuck, Sheena?" She had been agitated for an hour but now she made no attempt at hiding it.

"Don't!" was the only thing I could think to say, the only way I knew how to put it.

Rubbing her eyes, she said, "Don't what?"

"Go back there."

"It's where I live?"

I decided that speaking around it wasn't going to work at all. "You know what I'm talking about."

She closed her eyes and breathed deeply. "I have to," she said. I never heard anyone say something with as much sincerity.

"We can go somewhere else," I said running my damp hands down my jeans. "Take me somewhere else."

"Sheena…" she said, defeated.

"Anywhere," I said. "We can go to Graham Lake. It's not far, is it?"

"Stop it."

"If we go now we—"

"Sheena! Get me the fuck home!" Mom looked deeply remorseful the moment these words left her lips. I knew she didn't want to say them—*scream* them. But whatever hurt I felt from these agitated words changed immediately to my own rage. I was angry that I allowed myself to believe she was capable of anything more than a couple hours of amusement, that she had the strength to treat me like a daughter for any sustained amount of time. I was angry at her, but I was even angrier at myself for believing anything good could come out of this.

The car ride was completely silent. When she got home, she immediately disappeared into her private hell, locking the door behind her, without saying a word to me.

Chapter Ten

Mom was always sick when I was a kid. But it was a sickness caused by what she insisted on doing to herself—through the people she'd see, the places she'd go, it all led to her being passed out somewhere on a bed or on the floor, throwing up, and being impenetrable for hours, unable to be a real mother.

My eyes were opened on a night that began with another huge fight between her and grandma. I don't even remember what it was about and was too young to understand anyway, but they were screaming at each other in the snowy yard, looking like they wanted to hit each other. Neighbors kept opening their doors and peeping out their windows, and I watched, too, from the bedroom mom and I shared, nervous the police would come and take her away again.

Mom, who looked like she had enough, finally rushed into the house, grabbed her guitar, and shoved some clothes into a couple of bags; she dragged me out of bed, led me to the car, and we drove off. It wasn't the first time we left grandma's, but somehow, I knew we weren't coming back for a while this time.

I remember driving around for hours that night before finally pulling into a parking lot in a scary area of town where we slept in the car all night. Mom was on edge the whole time, and I didn't dare ask about all the other stuff we left at grandma's, not that we had much. But my school bag was there, so I figured we'd go back at some point once she calmed down. This time, we didn't go back; not the next day, or the day after that.

Instead, we spent two days driving around town for a place to stay or people to borrow money from, but no one ever seemed to be home. So, night after night, we slept in the car.

That is until the night we ran out of gas.

Mom pulled into a small, fenced in lot next to an old, rundown building that, to my young eyes, looked haunted. The car stalled as we rolled to a stop.

"Shit!" She said, lowering her head onto the steering wheel.

"What?" I asked.

"Out of gas…"

"Are we gonna get more?" I asked.

"How?" Mom said.

"At the gas station."

"With what?"

I didn't understand the question, so I just stared at her.

"No money, kiddo," Mom said, with tears running down her face. I can still remember how hopeless she looked.

"I have twenty-three dollars at grandma's," I said. "We could use that."

Mom shook her head. "We're not going back there."

"Never?" I asked.

She shrugged like she really didn't want to answer the question. I then saw her shaking, like she was scared or cold, or maybe both. I was scared and cold too, and I could feel my lips trembling. Mom stared out toward one of the creepy nearby buildings.

"I know someone who lives there," she said.

"That place looks scary," I said.

"It's not that bad," she said, opening up the car door. "Come on, get out."

I stepped out of the car and wrapped and held my old coat around me since the zipper was broken. Mom had an arm around me as we marched along the sidewalk, down a couple blocks, past what looked to me like one abandoned building after another. We then stopped at one doorway where mom looked down at me nervously before she opened the door and went inside. After going up three flights of stairs, we approached a door at the top and knocked.

"What are we doing here?" I asked stepping back. "I don't like it."

"Surviving," she said, almost under her breath.

No one answered the door, so she knocked again. Then again, harder. Finally, we heard the floorboards moan on the other side of the door. Someone was coming, but this someone didn't open the door. To me, it felt like we were being watched through the peephole for what seemed like forever.

Then we heard a voice: "Yeah, what?" It was the kind of voice you'd expect to hear on the other side of a strange door in a strange house, late at night. Raspy, unwelcoming. I couldn't tell if it was a man or woman's voice.

Mom got closer to the door. "Yeah…uh…is Kevin there?"

There was another pause. "Who is it?" This time the voice lilted a bit and sounded like a woman's voice.

"Ronnie."

"Who?"

"Ronnie...he knows who I am," mom explained. I could see she wasn't thrilled to be talking into a door.

Again, a pause, then: "Well, he's not here."

"Do you know when he'll be back?"

"No."

Mom stepped back from the door, clearly at a loss. I had no idea who this Kevin was but it seemed like she badly wanted to see him. She turned back around. Knocked again, even harder.

"Can you just open the door? Please?"

I didn't think it was going to happen, but after a pause, the door handle turned and the old scary door opened a few inches. The woman was there, staring at us from behind the door chain.

She looked about mom's age but certainly didn't look happy to still be dealing with two strangers at that hour.

"Look," the woman said, annoyed. "I will tell Kevin whenever he gets back you were—"

"Can we come in?" Mom said before the woman could finish her sentence.

"What?" The woman was surprised by mom's question.

"It's just we're having car trouble and it's cold and it's late..."

"Yeah, it's late...and we don't take vultures."

"Please, I'm not a vulture." I had no idea what a vulture was but mom pulled me close to her to convince the woman, daring the woman to turn away a kid.

The woman glanced down at me and said, "This isn't a place for kids. Trust me."

"I know exactly where I am," mom said. "Please."

The woman closed the door before mom could say another word. I figured we were going head back downstairs but then I heard the chain slide off and the door opened again.

"Fine." The woman gestured us inside, and I could instantly see what she meant. It was very dark, lit only by the light of a television, but I could still see how trashed the place was with fast food bags and pizza boxes, piles of clothes and empty soda and beer cans. Everything was junky and broken: chairs and couches that looked like they came from the dump, sleeping bags and mattresses scattered here and there. I was also hit by a strange odor of piss and cigarettes.

"I told you," the woman said, probably noticing my reaction. "Not exactly a place for little girls."

After looking more closely, the woman seemed older than mom, but in her tight jeans and black t-shirt, she was dressed like someone half her age.

As we moved in, I noticed that some of what I thought was laundry was actually people sleeping on the floor, at least three of them, just lying there on the worn hardwood. A guy a few feet away rolled over, snorted, and startled me closer to mom.

The woman giggled then said, "Could be a long night for a kid in here, you know."

"Don't worry," mom said.

"There's no telling when the hell Kev will be back. Could be tonight or tomorrow. Who knows? The shelter might a better option."

"We're not homeless," mom quipped.

"Got any money?" She asked. "Kev's not really generous these days if you're looking…"

"I said I'm not a vulture."

The woman stopped talking and got right up into mom's face. "Oh my God!" She said. "I know who you are! You were in that band from way back when, right?"

Mom nodded.

"I was a year ahead of you in high school. What were you guys called, your band?"

"The Legs."

"Right! Me and my sister saw you one time at that bar over on Pine. What happened to you guys? You went to New York, then what?"

"Nothing really."

"You had that song on the radio…what was it called?"

"It doesn't matter."

Mom never liked talking about her time in The Legs, and I was never sure why. My aunt, Kim, once said mom went to NYC one person and came back another. Whatever happened there, I'm told it brought her to a very dark place.

For whatever reason, this woman was much nicer suddenly. "I'm Carla," she said. "How do you know Kevin?"

"Probably for the same reason you do," mom said.

Carla smiled. "I got a blanket you can use, and there's an empty mattress over there."

"Thanks."

"And I can probably help you out with…you know." Carla looked down at me like adults do when they don't want kids to understand what they mean.

"I'll wait a bit," mom said, also glancing down at me.

A few minutes later, Carla offered us some pizza that looked days old and tasted even older, but I was starving and mom was desperate, so we didn't really care much how it tasted. Then, after an hour or so of mom only half listening to Carla ramble on—mostly about the people they went to high school with—we went over to the empty mattress, laid down, and tried to get to sleep. Carla disappeared into some room down the hall.

We laid there trying to keep warm, trying to ignore these strange floor people nearby who kept shifting around and grunting in their sleep. It took a while, but after twenty minutes of mom caressing my head, I felt my eyes getting heavy. Soon, I was asleep.

And I would have easily slept through the night but the sounds of whispers and moving chairs over in kitchen area woke me at some point, probably hours into the night. I opened my eyes. Mom wasn't near me. Scared, I looked around and saw her over at the dark kitchen with Carla, lit only by the glow of the street lights through the window just over me. Neither saw me watching as they hid in the shadows; I could see they were taking puffs from something that looked like a cigarette, only they were putting the tip of it against what looked like tin foil.

They did this a couple of times before leaning back in their chairs, both staring up at the ceiling with dead expressions. For five minutes, mom didn't move. I got scared and nearly went over to check on her, but then she suddenly looked around with half-closed eyes—still not noticing I was watching—and lowered her head onto the table and went to sleep.

Even then, in my cluelessness, I somehow knew mom had just put something in her that made her sick again. It still confused me. Why would she do it if it made her sick or fall asleep? Who wants to fall asleep all the time or not understand anything or people when they talk to you or fight all the time with people? This is what was happening with mom, all the time now, and I felt helpless to stop it.

The more I thought about it—lying there on some gross mattress in some gross apartment—the more it boggled me. And the more it boggled me, the more tired I got. And before I knew it, I was asleep again.

When I woke the next morning, I was alone. No mom, no Carla, no floor people. Just me in a cold apartment. I panicked a little and rushed over to the window to see if mom's car was still there, which it was. This was the first time I remember fearing abandonment. Did I really think mom was going to somehow get gas and drive away in the middle of the night without me? Not really. I still held the assumption—maybe a naive assumption—that all mothers wanted to be with their kids.

Mom was becoming unpredictable, though, and there was no telling what she would do next and why. And why the hell would she leave me, and leave me here in such a horrible place? It wasn't possible. Still, I panicked and ran into each trashy room, but there was no sign of her. I then ran out of the apartment, down the several staircases, and onto the sidewalk. Just then, a car pulled up. It was a loud, junky car. I stepped back as the passenger door opened. Mom stepped out.

"What are you doing out here?" She asked me.

"Looking for you."

"Well, here I am," she said as the car drove away.

"Where did you go?" I asked.

"I had to do a couple of things."

"Can we leave now?" I asked.

"Soon."

I wasn't sure if soon meant in an hour or next month, but before I had the chance to ask, mom took me back into the apartment. We didn't leave the next hour or the next day. That horrible apartment was becoming the place where we were living, and I hated every minute of it.

For one thing, there was almost nothing for me to do other than strum mom's guitar and occasionally play Ms. Pac-Man on this old-school joystick thing that you plugged directly into an ancient TV that had no cable. Over the next few days, I hung around the apartment as mom came and went. Where she went, I had no idea. But wherever it was, she'd come back with a different guy almost every night.

I just figured she was looking for a new boyfriend and working really hard to find just the right one. The one guy she seemed to be with the most turned out to be Kevin, the guy she originally came to see. He didn't say much, and mom was always handing him money, and he was always handing her little plastic bags that made her really, really happy.

One afternoon, though, she stormed into the apartment extremely *unhappy*.

"What the fuck, Kevin?" She hollered, slamming the door behind her.

She ran around frantically, checking each room. She then ran into the living room area and kicked one of the floor peoples' feet. "Who did it?" She screamed. "One of you junkies?" The three people lying on the floor rolled over and looked at mom, clueless. I was also clueless. Mom freaking out wasn't a rare thing exactly but now she seemed really pissed off, and I couldn't think of why.

"You gonna tell me?" Mom was furious.

Kevin came out of a room in a t-shirt and underwear, still out of it. "What, Ron?" He asked.

"Some asshole broke into my car, jacked my stereo and all my CDs," mom said, out of breath. "Broke me goddamn window!"

Kevin reached under his shirt and scratched his chest. "And you think it's one of them?" He gestured toward the floor.

"I don't know. Maybe."

Kevin was a tall, awkward looking guy with thick, black rimmed glasses. He had a pot belly but was skinny everywhere else, and he had a beard. Nothing seemed to bother him, certainly not mom's stolen car stereo, but he didn't seem too happy to be listening to mom rant. "It was only a matter of time in *this* neighborhood," he said, slightly annoyed.

Mom kicked one of the floor people again, a woman, who got up and shoved mom to the floor. "Don't fuckin' kick me!"

This woman, who smelled like she hadn't showered in years, went from comatose to raging in less than a second. "Why would I want your car stereo?"

Mom got up and rammed her back, and they began to clutch and grab each other. Kevin quickly stepped in and pulled them apart and said, "Hey, hey! Cut it out or you'll both have to bounce!"

Mom stormed out and didn't return until late that night, so I found a corner and played mom's guitar until she came back.

I soon learned that stealing—or suspecting others of stealing—was a regular occurrence there. Everyone who came and went at some point accused someone of stealing something from them: cigarettes, food from the fridge, jackets, money. It seemed like anything of value was up for grabs. Still, it never occurred to me to hide mom's guitar or to at least not leave it out in the open. Why would it? One morning, I woke up and didn't see it in its usual spot: by the window, leaned against the wall.

I ran across the room and back again, looking in every corner, behind every chair, under the kitchen table. No one was up yet, so I looked in a closet next to the floor people and in the one at the end of the hallway. Nothing. And though it terrified me, I began to open doors and searched into bedrooms while people slept, each of them looking dead to the world. When I opened the third and final bedroom door, I saw mom sleeping in a bed with Kevin. Next to her on the nightstand was a needle, and this time, I sort of knew what that needle did to her.

I closed the door gently. Her guitar was gone.

Days had gone by. Mom never mentioned her guitar at all or even noticed I stopped playing it. She rarely spoke to me. When mom was awake, which was becoming more and more rare, she'd see me in passing, ask if I was okay, and then leave with Kevin somewhere while I stayed in the apartment. Sometimes I'd leave and go for a walk. It was a scary neighborhood, so I stayed close to the apartment and always came home before it got dark.

There was really nowhere to go and not much to see—only a hole in the wall convenience store, a dive bar, and a little park with a few swing sets and a slide. Other than that, it was one rundown apartment after another. But I just had to get out and clear my head. As I walked, I thought a lot about school and wondered if my teacher missed me at all. I thought about mom's guitar and wondered who stole the thing.

At one point, I thought about using the old cordless phone in the apartment to call grandma, even picking it up one night while everyone slept. And even though it was really late, I probably would have called. But there was no dial tone.

One afternoon while I was walking, I decided to turn down a new street. Lost in my thoughts, I passed a pawn shop and just happened to notice a guitar displayed in the window. I stopped dead. It was mom's guitar. I knew it was. There was no mistaking the burn marks on the headstock from mom leaning it too close to a candle (at least that's what she once told me). I stood there completely at a loss. Someone, I had no idea who, stole mom's guitar and sold it. Was it Kevin? One of the floor dwellers?

People, all sorts of strange people, were in and out of that apartment all day. It could have been anyone. And the more I thought about it, the angrier I got.

I took a seat on a nearby bench and considered my options, which weren't many. Normal people would immediately go to the police with something like this, but I knew I couldn't because it would likely lead to mom getting in trouble. Explaining my situation to the store owner probably wouldn't do any good; he looked mean, and he probably had tons of stolen items in there. And since I had no money with me, there was only one option left. I just didn't know how to pull it off.

For the next couple of days, I kept coming back to the bench outside of the store, always breathing a sigh of relief when I saw the guitar still hanging in the window. As I sat there, I watched the store owner, a short, round man who rarely moved from behind the counter.

Sometimes, though, he'd disappear into a back room and come out with a box of items he would then display somewhere in the store. This could take a couple of minutes or a couple of seconds, and it was impossible to know when.

So one morning, around 10 am as the shop opened, I took my place on the bench and waited for my moment. The store owner spent the first hour or so opening mail and writing in a notebook. Now and then he'd type on a less-than-state-of-the-art computer on the counter. I was getting really impatient, and I nearly left. But as luck would have it, I heard a phone ringing from within the store.

I watched him look around like he was trying to find it; he then got off his stool as it kept ringing. I stood up and got closer, making certain he didn't see me. He then—just as I had hoped—went to the backroom. Without thinking or rationalizing it for a second, I busted into the store with no intention of being quiet—just fast. I ran to the window display, grabbed the guitar by the neck with both hands, and was out the door before the store owner had a chance to see what happened.

I sprinted down the block, not looking back once. There was no way the store guy was catching me but I still ran like my life depended on it, ignoring don't walk signs, arms wrapped around the instrument. I didn't stop until I reached the house where we were staying, and it felt weird to think of it as a safe place.

But it was far from a safe place, and I would be reminded of this when I got to the top of the stairs and opened the door. By chance or fate, mom was standing right there as though she was about to leave. Over her shoulder, I saw one of the floor people cradling another in her arms. She was holding him tightly and crying.

Catching a quick glimpse of his face, I saw that he was young—a teenager, probably, though he looked older than he likely was—and his eyes were open, but there was no life there. By the way the woman was crying, I knew he was dead, and by the way she was crying, I knew he had to be her son. There was a needle next to him.

Mom took my hand and led me downstairs. "We gotta go now," she said.

"Where?" I asked.

"Anywhere but here," she said.

I wanted to believe that mom took me away from that place because it was a bad place and that bad things happened there, things that a kid should never see. Looking back, it was probably more likely that she was running from trouble, a police raid perhaps.

As we were driving away, heading to who knows where, mom asked, "How did you get that?" I still had my arms around the guitar.

I didn't know what to say, so I said nothing. She then noticed the price tag still hanging from one of the tuning knobs. She smiled.

"Took it back, huh?"

It was then I realized it was mom who pawned the guitar. I guess she must have really needed the money.

Chapter Eleven

Mom didn't emerge from her room until late the next evening. I was on her couch flipping through my stack of old records, thinking seriously about going back to New Hampshire when her door finally opened. She emerged from the shadows like she was coming out of a tomb; her hair was knotted, her eyes half shut, and she was still wearing clothes from the day before. It was sad, for sure, but I was too pissed to feel too sorry for her. I wondered why she still had to wreck everything.

She sat next to me and slid a record from the top of the stack. "This one's great," she said. "Timeless."

The record was *Ziggy Stardust*.

"You like Bowie?" She asked.

Of course, I liked Bowie. Who doesn't like Bowie? But at that moment, I just didn't care, so I shrugged and gave her the silent treatment. I wanted her to know I was mad at her. Flipping the record cover over, she read the back to herself, or at least pretended to read it. My guess was that she was thinking about what to say. "Ever do something you hate doing, but you do it anyway?" She said, breaking the silence.

"Like eating an entire bag of chips in one sitting? Like sex with a stranger?" I answered.

Sensing my bitterness, mom put the album back on the stack and zeroed in on me. "Why did you come all the way up here, Sheena?" She asked. "Don't get me wrong, I'm really happy that you did. But why would you want to see me?"

"It's complicated," I said.

"I'm not blind about the shitty things I've done to you," she said, scratching her left arm. "And I can't even look at myself in a mirror now. Why would you, of all people, want to see me?"

Even though it seemed pointless, I decided to get real with her; so I pulled out the brochure from my coat pocket and shoved it into her hand.

After looking it over, she said, "Oh! Is this where you're going in the fall?"

I folded my arms. "I'm not holding my breath," I said. "College still costs money. Shit tons of it. And I have no money."

It took a minute but it soon sunk in. She looked up at me and said, "Hold on…you came up here to get money?"

I was stone-faced.

"And you think I have money?" She asked. "Why would you think that?"

"That's the rumor," I answered.

A look of realization came over her. "You talked to Aunt Laurie, huh?" It was all clicking now.

"Good guess," I said, tauntingly.

Mom looked a little hurt by this epiphany. "So this is why you're here now? For money?"

She nodded slowly, as though my random visit suddenly made sense now. "Well, as you can see, Sheena, I'm no Kardashian."

"Let me guess, you spent it all?" I took the brochure back. "On what? Oh, let me guess…" She was scratching her arms again.

"Jim handles my money, Sheena," she said. "I've never been good with that stuff. He got us this trailer."

This is when it became clear that Jim had total control over her and that whatever money she had went directly to him. I suppose this kind of helplessness would make some daughters pity their mothers, but it made me even more angry at her. How could she let it happen?

"So that meant more to you than helping your own daughter?" I said, really going for the jugular now.

"That's not fair, Sheena," she said.

"Not fair, Mom? Let me make that call. I happen to be an expert on what's not fair!"

"I gotta live somewhere."

"Must be nice. I'm currently living in my car as of yesterday."

"You can stay here for as long as you want. We have room."

"Why the fuck would I want to stay here?"

Mom was scratching the hell out of her arms now. "I thought you came here to see *me*," she said quietly, almost to herself.

"Are you seriously trying to guilt trip me? For real?"

Mom lowered her head and started to cry, and I could tell they were real tears, not the forced kind. "I'd like to help, Sheena. I really would. But…"

She wanted to explain why she couldn't but wept into a throw pillow instead. I knew why. Mom never really had full control over her life to begin with, and now it was in the hands of some asshole drug dealer. That was it. As pissed as I was, seeing her cry like this made me accept what I had sensed since I arrived. Mom was still very lost, and I wondered if it would ever change.

She focused on me and said, "I hope to god you never understand what this thing can do to you, and that it hasn't taken hold of you yet."

"What do you mean *yet*? What thing?"

"That demon."

"What demon?"

"The one that changes your brain and gets you hooked," she said. "That thing that turns you into everything you hate and makes you hurt everyone you love."

"What are you talking about? Why would it get a hold of *me*?" I asked, but I had an idea of what she was getting at.

"How many pills have you had today?"

"Just stop, Mom."

"You don't think I see it?" She said. "What are they? Xanax? Ativan? I know all about that stuff."

"Xanax," I said defensively. "So what? They're prescribed."

"That makes no difference."

"I'm not addicted if that's what you're thinking. Why are you changing the subject?"

"I know pain when I see it, Sheena, believe me," she said, drying her eyes with her palm.

For some reason, I felt the need to deflect. "I'm not fuckin' addicted!"

Deep down, I knew she was right. The pills didn't help much with my anxiety anymore. So why did I still take them and why was I taking so many now? I feared it was because I couldn't stop.

Now I really wanted to change the subject. Without a word, I started flipping through the stack of records, hoping we could talk about something else. It was a weird feeling, having my mother speak to me like she cared.

Several minutes passed before either of us said anything.

"Hold on," she said, perking up. She took the top album from the stack. "This one might work."

It was an album by The Kinks called *Something Else*. She held it and stared deeply into the front cover art which consisted of portraits of the band members and fancy lettering.

"Work? For what?" I asked.

"For the open mic," she said. "*Waterloo Sunset* is a beautiful song, and pretty easy to play."

Mom seemed serious about getting up in front of people and performing but I wasn't buying it yet. "Whatever," I said.

"Don't sound so encouraging!" She said sarcastically. "I'm really doing this, you know."

"That's great, Mom. I want you to do it, too—if that's what you really want."

"Will you help me?"

"How?"

"Get your guitar."

Reluctantly, I took out my guitar and we played into the night, listening to *Waterloo Sunset* over and over and over, rehearsing it over and over and over, with each pass growing more impressed at how good we sounded and how well our voices blended. Mom's was lower and raspy, and mine was higher, so I sang the harmony. It was just after 2 pm when she stopped suddenly.

"Will you get up there with me?" She asked like it was life or death.

"Where?" I knew what she meant but I still avoided the question.

"What do you mean where? On stage."

Maybe I should have jumped at the chance, but I didn't. "Why do you want me there?"

"We sound pretty good together, don't you? And it would be nice having someone there with me."

I smiled and nodded.

So for the next few days, we kept playing. Our sessions lasted hours, and we often lost track of time, even forgetting to eat on a couple of occasions. We tightened the harmonies and made the songs our own. We sounded great, and I felt great about performing. One night, we fell asleep next to each other, holding our acoustics, and slept through the night. But around 8 am, a car rolled into the driveway. It was Jim. Through the screen door, I watched him get out of his car and stumble up the stairs. He was obviously drunk.

"What's all this?" He said, opening the door and staggering in.

Mom woke and sat up. "What?" She asked.

For some reason, the word *what* really pissed him off. "*What?* You're asking me fuckin' *what*?"

"Chill out, Jim," mom said, trying to wake herself up.

He came closer. I could smell the beer on him from where I was sitting. "You ask me *what* like I don't live here. Are you kidding me?"

He looked directly at me, like I was an intruder. "Weird girl's still here?" he said.

"Shut up, Jim, you're hammered." Mom was fully awake now.

Jim erupted. "Now you're telling me to shut up in my own house?"

"Calm down!" She said, but he didn't calm down.

He got right in Mom's face and screamed, "In my own house!" again, then again. There was no way a neighbor didn't hear it.

Jim then took mom's guitar by the neck and lifted it waist high, threatening to smash it against the coffee table. Convinced he was really going to do it, I jumped up and clung to his arm. It wasn't hard to stop him because he was so drunk. He looked at me and started laughing. I had no idea what was so funny, but he nudged me away and threw the guitar onto the couch next to where mom was sitting. The asshole laughed all the way into the bedroom, slamming the door behind him.

By the night of the performance, we were very much ready. On the way over to the bar—a joint called The Grog—we warmed up by singing an acapella version of *Waterloo Sunset*, feeling super-psyched to play—that is until we finally pulled into the parking lot. Mom's mood shifted. She didn't get out of the car. She sat motionless, not saying a word.

"What's wrong?" I asked.

"I don't know."

"Don't tell me you're chickening out."

"Of course I am," she said, lighting up a cigarette.

"What the hell, Mom!"

The thing about mom is that she could be one way one minute and be something else the next. This is how it always was. It was like living with a thousand different people.

Mom took the deepest drag I had even seen anyone take. "It's not a big deal, Sheena. We'd only be playing in front of twenty drunks anyway."

"That's not the point!" I yelled.

"What *is* the point?"

I tried to come up with something moving or inspirational but nothing really came to mind, so all I said was, "Just doing it is the point! You gotta do s*omething*, right?"

She thought about it for a moment. "What if we screw it up?"

"We have it down," I said, feeling like her coach. "It'll be fine, Ma." *Ma?* Did I really just call her 'Ma'?

She nodded, as though she actually believed me. "Okay…let's do this."

We jumped out of the car and carried our guitars inside. The place was an old-school seaport pub with nautical decor everywhere including lobster traps hanging on the wall. The grumpy guy setting up the PA directed us to a sign-up sheet at the end of the bar. We went over, and looked at each other with nervous smiles. Mom picked up the pen and wrote *Pierced Girls* on the fifth line.

"What the hell does that mean?" I asked.

"Not a bad band name," she said. "I like it."

We sat down at one of the pub tables. Mom ordered a beer and I ordered a coke. Even though the place was half full, I could tell mom was wracked with nerves, and it wasn't long before she was scratching at her arms again.

"Need to smoke a butt?" I asked.

Before she could answer, someone called her name from across the room. "Shit," she muttered to herself.

A guy I recognized from the party from a few nights before was coming over. I remembered noticing how pink his face was.

"If it isn't Joan Baez!" He said, obnoxiously. "Haven't seen you here lately. Is that a guitar I see?" He was laughing like something was funny. I had yet to see this guy sober.

Mom barely looked at him. "Just hanging out."

"Is Jim here yet?" He asked before taking a swig of beer.

"Jim's coming?" Mom asked like it was the last thing she wanted to hear. I felt the same exact way.

The guy with the pink face laughed again. "Hell, yeah, he's coming. Dart night."

Mom muttered something under her breath. I didn't think she was going to go through with it now, but when the guy left, she went over to the sign-up sheet. So I shadowed her.

"Stop," I said, taking her arm, knowing she was about to cross off our names. "Who gives a shit if he's here?"

She paused and threw down the pen. "He's always around at the worst possible times."

I came right out and asked her: "Why don't you leave him?" I was taken aback by my own bluntness.

It seemed like she was trying to come up with a good answer, gazing at the floor, but she didn't. She just shrugged and said, "Don't know."

After that, we decided to tune up and relax until it was our turn to play. The first act was some doe-eyed college-aged dude singing a Dave Mathews' song. The second was a middle-aged woman basically doing a karaoke version of *Don't Stop Believing*. When the song ended, Jim staggered in and went straight to the other room where the other guys were shooting pool and playing darts. Mom looked away, hoping he wouldn't notice her, as if one of his friends wouldn't tell him she's here.

It was sad how noticeably more edgy she was since he walked in. When the second act finished, mom went outside to have her third smoke since arriving. She wasn't gone three minutes when Jim came up to me, beer in hand, and asked where she was.

"Smoking," I said, sneeringly.

Buzzed as he was, he sensed my angst. "Is she really going up there?" He said with a short laugh. "Have you heard her sing lately?"

"We both are," I said, defiantly. "We're both doing this."

"Ah…the Dixie Chicks," he said with a smirk.

I stared back at him blankly to show him how unaffected I was by his words. He smirked again and headed toward the entrance to look for mom, probably to give her shit about something, probably about me.

The fourth act went on—a singer-songwriter Dylan wannabe lamenting about war or something—and I started to get nervous after not seeing mom after fifteen minutes. How many smokes was she having? Just as I was getting up to check on her, Jim came in and headed to the pool room. Mom was not far behind. She sat down and immediately put her head on the table like she wanted to take a nap.

"You okay?" I asked.

"He's such a prick," she said. Her speech was slurred.

"Mom?" I didn't like what I was seeing. She didn't respond and could barely lift her head.

"I don't want to do this," she said.

I was getting pissed now. "Mom!"

"You can sing without me."

"I'm not getting up there without you."

While we bickered, the sound guy went to the mic and announced our new band name: Pierced Girls. An awkward silence followed as he and twenty-five patrons scanned the room for whoever was supposed to go on. He announced our name again.

"Mom?" I said, urging her to get up.

"Fuck it," she said, nearly falling off her chair. She picked up her guitar and stumbled her way toward the mic. I knew, right then and there, she did more than smoke a cigarette outside. I just knew Jim gave her medicine.

For a minute, I wondered if we could fake it. At one time or another, she must've performed while strung out. But then she dropped her guitar as she tried to put it on. The horrible atonal crash of strings and wood silenced the room and made everyone stare. She looked like a complete idiot, and I felt like a complete idiot, standing there next to her, watching a total train wreck happening. While laughing at her own clumsiness, she picked up the guitar and assured the audience that it was 'all good…all good'.

But it wasn't all good. After placing the capo on the wrong fret, she went ahead and strummed her out of tune guitar like her arm was asleep; and when I didn't think it could get any worse, she started singing, forgetting every other word, mumbling what she didn't remember. I was so disgusted, so shocked and embarrassed, that I could only stand and watch with a deep sense of shame.

After about a minute of this horror show, Jim and his friends came in from the other room. They were very loud and very drunk. Jim thought it would be fun to mock clap and dance around. His friends, of course, joined in.

Mom looked up from under her hair and stopped singing.

"Is it done?" Jim asked, clapping with the most drunken mockery he could muster. There was scattered laughter throughout the room and a little polite applause that was more out of pity.

Mom was numb but could still feel the hurt she was supposed to feel when humiliated in public. She backed away from the mic and fell over a small amp that was positioned a few feet beside her. She hit the floor hard.

At that point, I couldn't take it anymore. Right or wrong, I didn't help her up. Instead, I ran out of the bar holding my guitar.

Chapter Twelve

I have very few memories of mom playing her guitar, singing, or even listening to music. At some point—probably before I was born—the pure joy of it had left her. Her guitar was usually locked away in the closet, collecting dust. But that's not to say there weren't the occasional attempts at reawakening what was once her reason for living.

I'm not sure why, but around the time I was seven, mom had this sudden impulse to get back into a band, so she dragged me to some audition in Boston late one night. Since she and grandma weren't talking, there was no one around to watch me, so there I was, wearing pajamas under a winter coat, and sitting close to her on the underground train on our way into the city. I remember being awed by all the lights, the loud noises of the train and cars on the street, people everywhere.

And I could tell she was nervous—she barely said anything or even looked at me while the train carried us under the city toward our destination. When we finally arrived at our stop, she picked up her guitar with one hand, led me out of the train with the other, then up a flight of concrete stairs and onto the street.

"I'm not sure how long this will take," she said as we walked, "but you may need to sit by yourself for a little while."

"Where?" I asked.

"I don't know," she said. "Somewhere out of the way."

"Where are we going?" I asked.

"To an audition."

"What's that?"

"It's when you want to show that you're good enough for something."

"Good enough for what?"

"Playing guitar, singing. In a band."

"What's a band?"

Mom was trying to be patient with me but kept looking at a piece of paper and at the numbers above the doors. "A rock band, like a group of people playing cool music together."

"Do you think you're good enough?"

"I don't know," she said, rubbing her forehead. "I used to be."

After we marched by another block, it suddenly hit me. "I gotta pee," I said.

Mom halted and could not have looked more frustrated. "Shit. Of course, you do. Well, you're gonna have to hold it, or else we'll be late."

"I can't," I said, stopping in my tracks.

"Where are you gonna go?" She said, scanning around. "It's late and nothing's open." I tightened every muscle in my lower region and still managed to walk as mom pulled me down the sidewalk. We suddenly stopped when she found the right address.

"This is it," she said, taking deep breaths. It was an old brick building with a large metal door. There was no sign of anyone inside.

"Do they have a bathroom?" I asked, crossing my legs.

Mom may have been too nervous or distracted to hear the question because she said nothing as she sprinted up the steel staircase. There was a note on the door.

"Let's go," she said to me, pushing the door.

I followed her inside and down a dim hallway, hearing faint music getting louder as we walked closer. We stopped at another large door at the end of the hallway. The music was loud now, but the only thing I cared about was not peeing my pants.

"Wait here," mom said as she opened the door and went inside.

I didn't want to wait there. It was a creepy and cold hallway, and there was no place to sit and nothing to do, so I crossed my legs and leaned against the wall, hoping mom would only be there for a few minutes. When it was clear she wasn't coming out for a while, I decided to look around for a bathroom on my own, but every room was just one empty space after another. I finally went up a flight of stairs that led to another hallway that was even more dark and creepy. At the end of it was a light escaping from a partially open door.

Praying this was a bathroom, I hobbled, clenching every muscle, as fast as I could until I was at the door. I opened it and was relieved to see it was a bathroom, although it might have been the most disgusting bathroom I'd ever seen. Not caring in the slightest, I ran to the only stall, kicked open the door, only to see someone was in there.

I froze.

It was a woman, and she was so out of it that she didn't even notice me. In one hand, she was clutching a lighter; in the other, a pipe—the kind you smoke. I had seen one before. After a moment, with eyes half-closed, she slowly turned her head toward me. Without saying a word, I darted out and back down the hallway and down the stairs. I didn't care what mom was doing, I needed to get out of there, so I ran to the door where she left me—nearly peeing myself in the process—and forced open the door.

The loud music nearly knocked me over; there were speakers everywhere, guitar players, someone pounding on drums. In the middle of it, all was mom, strumming violently at her guitar, hair swinging all around her. I ran over and tried to get her attention. When she noticed me, her eyes widened and she gestured at me like she wanted me to go away. The other musicians watched, not sure what was happening.

Mom began to turn red when she saw I wasn't going anywhere, and I *wasn't* going anywhere. She was my mother and it was her job to get me to the bathroom. It was her job to get me out of that horrible place to somewhere safer.

She kept pointing toward the door but I kept shaking my head. By then, it was too late. I couldn't wait another second, so the piss flowed out of me, down my clamped legs, and out of the bottom of my pajamas. Some guy standing nearby noticed the puddle forming at my feet and practically leaped away like it was toxic waste. Then it became a scene as everyone in the room took notice—the drummer, the singer, the guitar player, and especially mom, who looked completely mortified.

Whatever embarrassment she felt quickly turned to rage as she took her guitar and slammed it hard with both hands on the concrete floor. It was as if all her anger and frustrations were put into this one destructive motion, and even then, I knew I was at the heart of this anger. In a way, she was throwing her guitar at me. And looking back now, smashing a guitar may not have been a huge deal—perhaps even encouraged—but the guitar bounced off the floor and hit one of the other musicians in the leg. Words were exchanged and soon mom was yelling every expletive she knew.

"What the fuck?" Someone said.

"Chill the hell out!" Another said.

Mom then elbowed a girl with pink hair—who looked half her age—into an amp. And after a few more shoves back and forth, mom ran out of the room as if I wasn't there, leaving her guitar, leaving me. If I didn't run after her down the street, following her down the cement staircase and onto the underground train, I probably would have been left behind.

When we entered our apartment late that night, mom went straight to bed without saying a word to me. And I'm pretty sure she never said anything about it again. She spent most of the following week in her room, so I knew she didn't pass the audition.

Chapter Thirteen

There was no way I was staying in that trailer overnight again. I was so pissed, I just had to leave, so I drove up and down the coast with no direction, no destination in mind. At one point, I nearly jumped onto the interstate to go home, to forget everything, including college. I saw the sign overhead: *95 South, Next Right*, and almost made the turn, but something held me back. It couldn't have been the money that I originally came here for (since I no longer expected it).

Maybe it was because I really had no home to go back to. Whatever it was—false hope, confusion, and concern for mom, whatever—I didn't get on the highway. Instead, I drove around for the rest of the afternoon and into the evening, popping Xanax, and feeling like a complete non-entity.

If I wasn't going back to mom's trailer, I had to get used to the idea of sleeping in my car for the foreseeable future. I remembered a Walmart in North Trenton which was as good a place as any to park and sleep, and maybe grab food after not eating for twelve hours. When I got there after a short drive, I was in and out with two protein bars and a chocolate milk.

But then, heading back to my car, I had the distinct feeling I was being followed. I even saw a shadow on the ground getting closer. Then, in the corner of my eye, I noticed someone was nearby.

"Yeah, it's her. It's definitely her," I heard a voice say; it was a deep, female voice.

"Piece of shit, white trash."

I whipped around and saw two women jogging toward me, each looked to be in their mid-twenties. I was sure they had me confused with someone else.

Now standing in front of me, ready for a fight, one asked, "Are you a shoplifter too, trash?"

"What the fuck are you—" Before I finished, I had it figured out. I knew exactly what was going on.

The other girl shoved my shoulder a couple of times, then started screaming at me like a psycho: "My mother breaks her back every day running our diner while junkies like you and that other old meth head chew and screw."

After a better look, I remembered her from the diner as one of the waitresses working behind the counter that morning.

"You can score pills and buy shit at Walmart but won't pay us for your fuckin' breakfast?" She shoved me again, this time much harder and in the chest.

Convinced I was about to get my ass kicked over pancakes and eggs, I tried to talk my way out of it: "I thought she paid, honestly! I really didn't know!"

"Bullshit," the other girl said.

"I swear to God," I said, pulling out my last twenty-dollar bill and holding it out. The one who kept shoving me snatched it and pushed me one last time. This time, I stumbled backward over a median, onto my ass. When hitting the pavement, my pill bottle tumbled out of my pocket and rolled toward them, stopping next to their feet. Before I could do a thing about it, the girl who kept shoving me glared and giggled as she lightly kicked my pill bottle into a nearby sewer grate.

"Don't come back," she said as they pranced away very pleased with themselves.

I wanted to push her back, to tell them to fuck off, even if it meant getting my ass kicked. But instead, I looked helplessly through the sewer gate for my pills, shining my phone light down into the black water, and saw the bottle floating in filth, far from my reach. Like an idiot, I tried to lift the grate, knowing it was pointless. Even if lifting it was a possibility, was I going to seriously jump ten feet down into sewer water to get them? Was I that hooked? If I was honest with myself, I probably was.

My mind started racing as I sat on the pavement. The thought of not having my pills within reach scared the hell out of me. I had nothing in my pocket to hold onto. Prescribed to me a year before by my doctor, they were always there when I started to get these relentless panic attacks, mostly at school. At first, I was using them only as needed, maybe a couple of times a week at most, but, soon, it was not enough. Not even close—I always needed more.

Aware of the signs, my doctor cut me off when I kept hounding him for more refills at a higher dose, so I had to go to the street. Every now and then, I would go without—sometimes hours, sometimes a day or two—like when I left them at home or couldn't score. And these stretches were never fun. I tasted the hell of withdrawal one day when I went to school and forgot them. By lunch, I had the shakes and wanted to rip my own skin off. My brain was pounding and everything felt like a threat.

I left school in the middle of a calculus test, just so I could take a couple of pills. This trial run of what withdrawal feels like made me dread the idea of ever stopping completely. When they weren't in my system, I simply wasn't myself. How bad would it be if I just suddenly stopped? This wasn't something I wanted to find out.

I got up and went to my car thinking about my options. Did no pills mean I was leaving Maine and to go home to see my supplier? Was there someone around who could set me up? Whatever the case, nothing was going to happen tonight, so I reclined my seat and tried to calm my racing mind by reciting lyrics and deep breathing. Maybe, just maybe, I'd feel normal in the morning.

I woke up hours later to the screeching brakes of a tractor trailer rolling into the parking lot. Wiping the drool off my mouth, I sat up and realized I felt far from normal, like I was about to die of the flu. I rolled down the window and sucked in as much cool morning air as possible, but what I really needed was water. I staggered out of the car, struggled to gain my balance, and dragged myself back into Walmart.

The store lights, the PA announcements, the banging shopping carts made me want to rip my eyes out of my head, but I somehow fumbled my way to a drink cooler, reached in, and immediately downed two bottles of water. Realizing I gave that waitress what was left of my money, I casually made my way toward the door and left without paying, feeling too horrible to care. As I hobbled through the parking lot, I glared at the people who watched me, this weird looking chick with green hair and a pierced nose, who looked like she just crawled out of an open grave.

In the car, I tried to breathe deeply, to use all that mindfulness shit, but none of it worked. I was too messed up. Hurting too much. As the light of the sun washed over the Walmart parking lot, I looked up at my face in the rear-view mirror, and for the first time ever, I noticed in my eyes a slight resemblance to mom.

Chapter Fourteen

Even in the moment, I knew it wasn't a good idea to drive fucked up. But I did anyway, hoping to ignore the hell I was in, but it was impossible to think about anything else but my pain.

It shouldn't have been a shocker when my eyes went blurry, and I lost control of my car along a sharp curve. Narrowly missing a tree, I went off the road completely and managed to get both right tires stuck firmly in a muddy embankment. It wasn't too steep but enough to prevent me from going anywhere. I gassed it several times, lurching forward a little each time, but it was hopeless. I stumbled out of the car, kicked dirt onto the road, and shouted, "Fuck me!" to the overcast sky. If this wasn't rock-bottom, it sure felt like it.

Ten minutes later, I tried again, revving the engine, and spinning the tires, but it became obvious I wasn't going anywhere without a tow or push. Giving up, I put on my hazard lights and wondered how long it would be before someone would drive up and take pity on me. For at least ten minutes, I paced up and down the road, shaking, deciding if I wanted to wave the next car down for help or jump under it.

At last, I heard one coming around the bend in the road—it was an old white pickup slowing down. It pulled over behind my car. Inside, I saw a couple of guys who looked to be in their thirties. It was dark but I could feel them staring at me, sizing me up for some strange reason. Judging from nets and lobster cages in the back, I was sure they just got off a fishing boat.

One guy jumped out. "You alright, kid?" He asked, strolling over in dirty jeans held up by suspenders. "Stuck?"

I did everything I could to not look like I was bugging out, but I felt so terrible that it had to be obvious that something was wrong with me. "Yeah, I'm a total idiot," I said with a nervous giggle.

"But you're okay?" He asked, again, stepping over to my car.

"Yeah, I'm fine."

"Shit, look at that. You're stuck as hell," he said, crouching down next to my back tire which was half deep in mud.

"Yeah, really fucking stuck," I said, not sure why I felt the need to swear.

I felt paranoid; he kept looking at me as if trying to determine whether or not I was on something. The other guy was still in the car, slurping out of a fast food cup, and guessing by the smell, smoking a joint. He came out eventually and strutted over.

"She wasn't texting, was she?" He asked.

"No…I just lost control," I explained. "It was dark."

The guy with the joint looked down at the stuck rear tire. "She ain't getting out of there without a tow," he said, quite sure of himself.

"Nah, we got this," said the other guy. He then told me to get in the car and give it gas when he signaled.

I did what he said and waited for the signal. When he gave the thumbs up, I gassed the shit out of it. It took four or five attempts with the car rocking forward and back, dirt spraying everywhere, but they managed to push the car back onto the road. Relieved, I pulled over to the side, drenched in sweat, my heart pounding like crazy. I got out and went over.

"I really appreciate the help," I said. "I don't know what I would've done."

"No worries," the nicer of the two said.

"No texting while you're driving," said the other who flicked his roach onto the road.

"I honestly wasn't texting," I reiterated.

As they turned and headed back toward their truck, I blurted out something I would have never said in my right mind: "Do you know where I can score pills?"

They both looked at each other. I put my head down and was immediately embarrassed.

"So that's how this happened?" The guy who had the joint said.

"Look, I'm not on Oxy or anything, just anxiety meds. I lost my pills," I said, hoping to convince them I wasn't some horrible junkie.

"Anxiety meds?" The first guy said.

I paused. "It's just that I'm not from around here and can't call my doctor."

The other guy smiled and knew he was being lied to. "Why do you think we'd know who to call for that shit?"

I didn't want to be insulting, but yeah—they sure looked like guys who would know someone I needed, and they had to get their weed from somewhere. I said, "I smelled the weed and thought you might know someone."

They kept looking at each other, smirking. "Maybe we don't, maybe we do."

"Can this be a *maybe you do*?" I asked. "Please." I was pretty much begging at this point. They continued to look at each other like they were conferencing telepathically.

The nicer guy took out a flip phone which was probably older than me. "Text this number. Maybe you'll get lucky."

I took out my phone and entered the number he read to me.

"Tell him Wally sent you. That's me." He closed his phone and slid it back into his pocket.

"Wally, okay, got it," I said. "I really appreciate this."

"He's slow to return texts sometimes, but he'll get back to you, I'm sure."

The other guy still looked grumpy, like he didn't trust me for some reason. "And don't be driving when you're on that shit."

At this point, I wanted to dash back into the car, but even in my current state, I didn't want to come off as ungrateful or anything. My restlessness, my crippling anxiety, was growing worse by the minute, and they saw this.

"Why does a kid your age need anxiety meds?" The first guy asked. "When I was your age, I didn't have a care in the world. What's there to worry about?"

I did everything I could to not bite his head off, even though I wanted to. "Things are different now."

Both laughed at me.

I thanked them again and drove off. They followed for about two miles before veering off onto a backroad. My mind was fixated on one thing now: getting pills and swallowing lots of them at once. This level of desperation worried me more than my normal, everyday anxiety. As each minute wore on, the more I hungered for my pills—the more I craved the comfort they gave me. I pictured myself taking them. Taking three, four, five at once. I was terrified of my lust.

Was mom right? Was I hooked? Was I a drug addict, too, like her? Could I stop myself if I really wanted to? Was I really about to text some random drug dealer in Maine?

I didn't even try to stop myself, though. Instead, I pulled into the first gas station, took out my phone as fast as I could, and sent that text:

'Lking 4 Xanax. Wally said u can hlp. THX'.

I then sat and stared at my phone as my body ached like hell. But what was going on in my head was infinitely worse. No matter how hard I tried, I could not control the racing thoughts, the hopelessness, my ability to feel normal. There was nothing, no positive thought, no prayer that could comfort me. There was no escape. Nothing helped. Just the hope of swallowing pills.

The instant my phone lit up, I picked it up and tapped on the new text message. It read:

'How many? 3 each. 20 minimum'.

This was more than I was used to paying, but what choice did I have if I was planning on sticking around? I shot back a text:

'Need 40. Where? ASAP'.

I felt unbelievably desperate and pathetic, but I wanted to stop the shaking, the tremors that wouldn't cease no matter how hard I tried. I wanted to feel normal again and didn't want to endure another minute of this torment.

Another text came in:

'1 hr. Trenton Dennys. What kind of car?'.

An hour? I took a deep breath and typed:

'06 black Civ. Ramones sticker. THX'.

On my way back to Trenton, I stopped at an ATM at some random bank to take out $120, only to realize that my recently deposited check from the bakery had not gone through yet, making my account balance a pathetic negative $37 along with an overdraft fee. I stood in the walk-in ATM about ready to pull a nutty, realizing I was beyond penniless and had no way of paying the guy I was supposed to meet in an hour. My options were zero, just like my bank account.

As I walked to my car, I had an idea, recalling the stash of money hidden in Jim's guitar. For about five minutes I sat in my Honda wondering if I was desperate enough to steal money from my mother's boyfriend. It didn't take long for me to decide that I was, so I started the car and headed to mom's trailer.

It was late afternoon by the time I arrived. I parked my car in my usual spot at the side of the road and got out, happy to not see Jim's car anywhere. Like a prowler, I entered the unlocked door and tiptoed across the trailer. As expected, mom was in bed, completely passed out as I crossed her room toward the closet. Quietly, I pulled out Jim's skull guitar case, making sure mom didn't move a muscle as I opened it. I reached inside and pulled out a roll of money.

The entire time, even though it was Jim's, I felt like another person. A bad person. Still, I went through with it, pocketing more than enough cash before returning the guitar case. Before leaving, I paused at the foot of mom's bed so I could see her breathing.

When I rolled into the Denny's lot, I parked in the far corner spot where I could be easily spotted. For an hour, I scanned the lot, and just as I started to think I was being blown off, I heard a tapping on my window. A guy was outside. I unlocked the car, allowing this complete stranger to get in, something I would have never done in my right mind. It took me a moment to realize, though, that the guy who got in was not a total stranger.

Sitting there, staring at me with a devilish smirk, was Jim. If I was feeling more like myself, I would have screamed. And even though I wanted to claw his face off, I sat there frozen, horrified. I was trapped.

"I knew it was you," he said, still smirking. "I just knew it. Not many Ramones fans anymore. Not around here anyway."

He then started the creepiest rendition of *Blitzkrieg Bop* imaginable: "Hey ho, let's go… Hey ho, let's go." Singing with his eyes closed and drumming on the dash, he was definitely mocking me. Still in shock, I didn't say anything. I just wanted him to leave so I could drive away and never come back. But he didn't leave. He stared into me, knowing how creeped out I was, enjoying every minute of it. The whole thing was so messed up.

His smile suddenly disappeared. "You couldn't have come at a worse time," he said with more than a hint of anger.

I wanted to tell him to fuck off and mind his own business, but I wasn't sure exactly how crazy the guy really was. He was more than your typical lowlife piece of shit who deals drugs; he beats up women, so who knows what he was capable of doing to me in an empty parking lot at night. I was reckless at times but I wasn't going to take that chance.

"Your mother is a sick woman," he continued. "Mentally, physically, you name it. She's got issues you can't even imagine."

I remained expressionless, and this seemed to irritate him even more.

"You have no idea how much you've messed her up by coming here," he said.

Still nothing, but I could feel myself shaking, and I knew he noticed.

"Fuck, you *are* hooked on this shit," he said. He then pulled out a pill bottle from his jacket and shook it. "When this stuff gets its fangs into you, it's almost as bad as heroin." Without a word, I took out the cash and held it out. I didn't care how sad the whole situation was, or how low and pathetic I felt. I wanted those pills and didn't care.

"Look," he said. "I know you came all the way up here to squeeze your mother for some money. That's pretty messed up—just appearing like that because you caught wind that she came into some cash. Fuckin' sad."

Being shamed by a drug dealer was pretty surreal. I didn't want to put up with it for another second. "Take it," I said. "Please." I couldn't have sounded more desperate.

He dropped the pill bottle into the cup holder, and said, "Keep the money. There are ten pills in there. Enough to get you home. The way you're going, they'll barely last you a day."

"I asked for forty," I said.

"When those are gone, that's it," he said. "I'm the only guy who can get those around here. You might as well head home now."

I turned away and looked out the window. The lot was filling up with mostly old people looking for their senior specials. My eyes were welling up now, but I didn't want him to see that he got to me. I barely knew this guy, but at that moment, I hated him more than I hated anyone. Why did he want me out of there so badly? I guess to a second-rate street pusher, to a parasite like him, I was a threat.

"I don't care about that money anymore," I told him.

"Then why are you still here?" He asked.

I didn't answer him. Why would I? My being there was none of his business. And as much as I hated him and wanted him to go, I hated myself more.

Jim opened the door and got out, but before closing the door, he stooped down and said, "If you give a shit about your mother, you'll go. She wants you to leave."

I didn't believe him. Now I really wanted to tell him to go to hell, but before I could, he slammed the car door and disappeared.

Will she realize she is as bad as her mom?

Chapter Fifteen

I didn't have many—what they called in school—'life skills'. But one I did have, and it wasn't a skill taught in any curriculum, was recognizing my own limitations, and I had many. I never had a problem knowing when I was completely screwed. Believing it was one of these occasions, I swallowed just two pills and started back toward New Hampshire, driving southbound on the long coastal road, all the way to the ramp and onto the interstate. By now, the pills got me close to normal, but they did nothing for the hopelessness in my mind.

What exactly was I headed back to? Other than my job at the bakery, I really had nothing in my so-called home town worth coming home to. Ok, I knew a few people, but not one would lose sleep if I just disappeared. The more I thought about it, the more I realized that it wasn't money that kept me looking back toward Maine. College was beside the point now; which was nothing new—it was always beside the point.

I was running away from something more important. Why was I running then? Was I really that hooked? For a brief time, I felt the torment of withdrawal and confronted the person I was when I didn't have my fix. I understood, really understood, on some level, what kind of demon had a hold of mom. If what I felt that day was any indication of the hell my mother was in, how could I possibly leave her now?

I'd like to claim that I immediately followed my instinct and turned right around, but I didn't. Instead, I spent the next couple of days living out of my car, wandering around random seaport towns in a constant state of pain and emotional paralysis. I went back and forth in my mind between forgetting about her forever and going back for reasons I may never understand. One afternoon, as I felt particularly awful, I headed toward the highway with every intention of leaving, thinking I would probably be better off putting all this behind me by heading southbound.

But before I turned onto the ramp, I felt utterly nauseous, so I pulled over into a grassy clearing not far from the water. Immediately, I opened the door and vomited into the dirt. When finished, I looked up and saw the skinny, towering figure of dad, leaning against the front of my car, peering at me from behind his shades, smirking. With the tugboat-filled harbor behind him, he couldn't have looked more out of context.

Ain't withdrawal a fuckin' drag? he said.

He came over and knelt in front of me. I looked up at him.

I've seen that look many times. I've seen it in my own face. It sucks, kiddo, I know.

"I'll be fine," I said, gagging on my own vomit.

Yes, you will, he said, standing up again. *We're survivors. But what about your mother?*

I wiped my mouth and rested my head against the door. "What about her?" I said.

He turned and gazed out toward the water. *There's usually only one ending to this story. I've seen it many times.*

I knew what he meant, and I knew he was probably right.

"So you're saying there's no hope for her?"

That depends on which road you get on.

"So this is on me?"

Sometimes you gotta take back what's yours. And don't forget to push over anyone in the way.

I stuck my head out again and puked some more. When I looked up again, dad was gone. After a few deep breaths, I drove off and took the north ramp back toward Trenton. As I drove, I hoped something would come to me—some way of getting her out of there. But the addict within her was exactly where she wanted to be. But deep down, as a mother, I had to believe she wanted out.

But what exactly could *I* do about it? Could I possibly convince her to leave? Maybe kidnap her? Killing Jim was an enticing idea but life in prison was not something I could stomach. No real plan revealed itself as I drove over the bridge back into Maine. But even though I was at a loss for what to do, knowing I was barely able to take care of myself, I still felt I needed to be there.

I crossed into Trenton, totally paranoid, scanning all over the place for any sign of Jim's car. I was irritated at myself for being *this* afraid of such a sad little man. I've seen parasites like Jim before; guys like him are always working some angle, always trying to suck something out of someone. I was convinced he was clinging to my mother for two reasons.

One: her recent cash hoard. Jim was a low-level drug dealer and was probably always scrounging for cash. Two: a guy this creepy could never get anyone as pretty as mom, who, though way past her prime, was still hot for her age. Indulging her addiction was the only way he could ever get her to hook up with him. The more I thought about it, the more I realized he was keeping mom hooked on drugs for his own messed up, insecure reasons. With a guy this sick, my fear of seeing him was completely reasonable. This presented a problem: How was I going to see mom without him seeing me?

When I was about a half-mile away from the trailer park, I decided to park my car in a small roadside clearing that didn't seem to belong to anyone. I then began creeping up the road, ducking into the weeds, behind trees, whenever I heard an oncoming car. Suddenly, I heard someone yelling at me: "Hey!"

I looked around and saw a guy marching toward me. He looked like one of Jim's loser friends.

He yelled, "Hey!" and nodded upward like he wanted to talk to me. "You headed over?"

"Where?"

"The hospital." He said this like it was the obvious answer.

"What? Why?"

An *oh shit* look came over his face. "Crap. You don't know?"

"Know what?" I started to prepare for the worst.

He paused, then said, "Your mom…she's in the hospital."

"What?"

"Yeah, she passed out a few nights ago."

I froze. And though it shouldn't have been a surprise, I still felt stunned.

"What happened?" I asked.

He looked away and said, "I think she partied a little too hard and, you know—" I could tell he didn't want to come clean.

"What happened? Tell me?"

He stammered, so I pushed him and screamed, "Tell me!" as he stumbled backward, looking shocked and even a little afraid.

"Take it easy, kid," he said, regaining his balance.

"Tell me now!"

"It was the H," he said. "A mild overdose, I guess."

Sure, I thought. This is exactly how it's supposed to go. Part of me knew this day was coming—the day I'd find out mom collapsed somewhere. I just didn't think I'd be around for it.

"She's alive though?" I asked, fully prepared for the worst.

"Yeah, she's alive. They're letting her out today. It could have been a lot worse."

A sense of relief fell over me. It wasn't too late.

"So she's coming back here today?" I asked.

"Yup. Jim and me are heading to the hospital in a few to pick her up."

I turned and got back into my car, trying not to appear like I was in any rush. In reality, every cell in my body was going haywire, and maybe I wasn't in the most rational state of mind, but I decided on the spot I was going to get her. *We* were leaving. *I* was picking her up. After all, I was her getaway driver.

Within ten minutes, I pulled into the hospital parking lot and parked in the closest empty spot, which apparently belonged to a physician. I sprinted through the automatic doors, getting a cross-eyed glare from the lady at the front desk who very suspiciously told me mom's room number and directed me toward the elevators. I kept looking over my shoulder as I went into the elevator and after I got out on the third floor, nervous that Jim would be close behind.

When I got to her room, mom was sitting on her made bed, dressed in her regular clothes, her bag next to her. I stopped at the door and hesitated. Was I really going to kidnap my own mother? Was this really going through my head? Was I thinking clearly? Then I thought, if she agreed to go with me, it wasn't kidnapping at all. But even if she didn't agree, I wasn't going to let her go back with Jim, even if I had to drag her out by the hair and take her far away.

I stepped into the room. "Ready to go?" I asked like it was the most normal thing in the world.

She looked up and was very confused. "Sheena?"

"Sheena. Right."

"Where?" She asked.

"Somewhere else that's not here," I said.

She looked around like she was trying to remember a prior conversation that never took place. "I thought…"

"Nope," I said, picking up her duffle bag and putting it around my shoulder. "There's only me."

"I thought Jim…" she protested.

Before she could finish, I said, "I don't give a shit about Jim. Let's go."

"Sheena…" She didn't move.

I glared at her with a look that defied her not to listen to me. "We don't have time to argue. Let's go!"

Mom was slow to get up, but once she did, she smiled and decided to trust me. Hand in hand, we hurried out of the room and into the elevator. Moments after she checked herself out, we were out the door and in my piece of junk Honda.

Chapter Sixteen

Once again, I was mom's getaway driver. Only this time, it meant something different, something more. This was a prison escape, and I realized during our silent car ride that this was just the beginning, that mom's true prison was herself. Running from a place was easy, but you can't run from yourself. And then it occurred to me that I was in my own prison, too. We were linked now—two addicts running away, together, with no direction.

After an hour of driving, mom asked the obvious question: "Are you gonna tell me where we're going or is this like a guessing game?"

I had no answer at first, but the more I thought about it, there was only one place that made sense, and it was the last place I remember us being happy and somewhat normal together, Graham Lake. Going there remained the one memory I could cling to, and now, being so close, it made sense to go there again.

I answered Mom with "You'll see," which seemed to satisfy her.

The road soon took us beyond the thick woods toward the shore of Graham Lake, and although it had been years since I'd been there, everything felt familiar. The lake was still untouched and exactly as I remembered it; the water was a pane of perfect, silver glass met by a shore made up of an infinite number of tiny round stones. Just a few feet from the water there was a row of rustic old cabins that, to my memory, had only the basics: two beds, a table and chairs, a faucet, and a toilet that was little more than a hole in the floor.

It wasn't part of some scheme or anything, but I started to believe we needed to be as far from any madness as possible.

Away from Jim. Away from all the drugs. Away from everything, except each other.

While mom slept, I pulled off into a gap in the trees and got out of the car. I then went into a small office and—with the cash from Jim's guitar case—paid the old man at the counter for seven nights in blind faith, not knowing if a week was too long or not nearly enough time for whatever it was we needed to do. I requested number five, which was *my* cabin, *our* cabin from when I was little, which also happened to be vacant. I drove over and parked with mom still sound asleep.

I turned off the engine and sat there looking out across the water, taking in the serenity of a place that hadn't changed a bit, even though we had. As each minute passed, I could feel the withdrawal tearing into me more fiercely than ever, and I wondered how long this hell would last.

After a half hour or so, mom opened her eyes and sat up. It only took a moment before she realized where she was, and when she did, she smiled as though it made total sense to be there.

I took out my pills and ached for them, wanting to devour each one. I clutched the bottle as I got out of the car, as the tremors started to come on. I had to move and distract myself somehow. It was about trying to survive the next moment as the numbness wore off and pain deepened. Mom followed and was as slow and feeble as ever.

We stumbled our way to the rocky shore, two junkies with nowhere to turn but toward the stillness and calm of a lake. We took in its beauty. Mom took my hand and squeezed it. I felt hope in her touch even though the darkness of withdrawal was waiting for us. I then threw the pill bottle into the lake. Faint smiles of exhilaration graced our faces.

"It won't feel good for long," she said running her hand through her hair. "I've tried to quit many times."

I watched the pills float on the still surface. I felt an impulse to wade out and get them but I suppressed it.

"How long?" Mom asked.

"How long what?" I wasn't sure what she was asking.

"How long you've been on those?"

"Too long."

Mom nodded her head. "That's long enough," she said.

She then reached into her bag and pulled out a little bag of powder. Her medicine. After a slight hesitation, she kicked off her sandal and waded in up to her knees in the lake. With her teeth, she tore open the bag and sprinkled the dust into the cool clean water. Following her in, I put my arm around her as we watched the powder dissolve.

"This is gonna hurt fucking bad," she said placing her arm around me. "Really bad."

"Fuck it," I said looking directly into her eyes. "Let it hurt."

Mom stepped timidly back onto the rocky shore. I could see fear in her eyes—as though she knew the darkness we were entering, a darkness she had yet to pass all the way through.

"Promise me something," she said, sternly, like a real mother.

"What?"

"Don't let me out of your sight."

"Ok…?"

"Seriously. Don't believe me when I tell you I'm running an errand, or just buying cigarettes, a soda, or a pack of gum. Assume I am lying to you. Because I will be."

I nodded.

"Don't believe me when I say some friend is coming over to drop off clothes, food, whatever. That will be a lie. That friend will have medicine. Nothing else."

I nodded again.

"Those lies won't be because I don't love you or anything like that," she said holding my both hands. "It won't be *me* lying. Please believe that."

I tried to make sense of what she was saying. I really did. And although I didn't understand her entirely, I accepted it and said, "Do the same for me, okay?"

She squeezed my hand as we walked along the shore and into our musty old cabin. I took it all in, overjoyed that it hadn't been updated in the slightest. We brought in what little belongings we had and settled in. I remembered the record player was in the trunk, so I brought it in and played *The Rise and Fall of Ziggy Stardust* in the kitchen area while mom rested in her small bedroom.

After an hour or so, we decided to walk down the road a mile to a nearby country store where we stocked up on bread, peanut butter, Ramen noodles, and a few bottles of generic soda. As we plodded back, I noticed mom was shaking, and it was more extreme than usual.

"You okay," I asked.

She forced a smile. "Not really," she said. "It gets a lot worse before it gets better."

She lit a cigarette. "You feeling it yet?" She asked.

I was trying not to think about how I felt. Whenever I did, I felt infinitely worse, so I always tried to change the subject in my mind. Sometimes it was impossible. But in order to give mom an accurate answer, I took a quick inventory:

Headache…check.

Nausea…check.

Tremors…check.

Anxiety…check.

Dread and hopelessness…not quite yet.

I forced a smile of my own. "You're right, it's not easy."

She took my hand as we made our way around the bend in the road. The sun was setting in the trees. When we got back, we put the groceries in the one cabinet, decided we were both exhausted and went to bed.

I didn't fall asleep right away; I could hear mom tossing and turning in the next room for well over an hour. Then, suddenly, everything was silent. Too silent. I could almost hear my thoughts like they were a freeform monologue for some crazy Netflix show. Soon, my irrational fears returned—the ones that never seemed so irrational.

What if I went crazy? What if I lost control? What if I'm a hopeless addict? What if there's no point to life? What if? What if? What if? For as far back as I could remember, I worried about things. Everything. Now, the Boogie Man under the bed had me by the neck with his arm extended and I couldn't push him away.

After another hour of agonizing, I fell asleep from pure metal exhaustion.

An hour later, though, I woke to the sound of my mother moaning on the other side of the thin wall. I jumped up and ran in. She was convulsing in a cold sweat, like she was possessed by a demon. I shook her, but it did no good at all. With arms wrapped around her, I held her close, trying to keep her from falling off the bed. But it seemed like her body needed to jolt, to purge.

Over the next few minutes, she calmed then convulsed again, clenching the sheets, crying, snorting air. This lasted about two hours before she was able to settle and drift back into a deep sleep.

I kept watch for a little while until I was reasonably sure she was okay. With all the adrenaline surging through me, there was no way I was going back to sleep, so instead went outside for some fresh air. Dawn was breaking, and I did everything I could to take in its beauty, the pure oneness of everything: the mist on the still water, the faint glow of early morning, and the chirps of cricket fading into those of birds.

But all this beauty seemed a little lost on me. I knew it was all beautiful. But for some reason, I couldn't feel it. As much as I tried, I couldn't take it in as much as I wanted to. I only recognized it intellectually. Now I had my own terror inside of me. I wasn't about to flail and convulse like mom, but there was deep restlessness, a unique kind of helplessness I had never known before. So this is what real withdrawal is like?

Remembering the only thing that always saved me—music—I went back inside and stood over the record player. I opened it like it was something holy, like it contained magic and divine truth. While mom slept in the next room, I took a record, not knowing which one, and placed it on the turntable. I lowered the needle and took in three seconds of slight hiss, then, out came a steady, echoing drum beat, a frantic bass line, followed by a monotone vocal howl singing:

I've been waiting for a guy to take me by the hand. Could these sensations make me feel like a noble man?

Honestly, I didn't love it, not immediately, at least. Whoever it was sounded like they were still taking lessons. It was archaic, but it didn't matter. Soon, after listening again, I found it beautiful, like a primitive painting. It was exactly what I needed.

As the first track ended, I didn't notice mom entering the room.

"Joy Division," she said in a rasp, startling me. "Keep listening, and you won't be able to stop."

We listened more. Then mom began giving a full lecture on the album and the short tragic history of the band's lead singer who hanged himself in his kitchen when he was just twenty-three. And you could hear the deep pain in the music like it was an audio suicide note, and I was impressed that mom knew every word, every note as she pointed out every nuance. But when the last song ended, she got real quiet, and soon, the tremors took over again, and she returned to her bed.

Over the next few days, this became a ritual. We would spend much of the day and night shivering, anguishing through the indescribable pain of withdrawal, trying (mostly in vain) to sleep as much as possible. Our main distraction was my record player. We went through each album from the stack, and mom, my teacher, would present full dissertations. Sometimes we'd get through it. Other times, she'd say 'I can't now' and would go to her room and face her demon.

One morning as mom slept, I realized something about her cannon of classic albums: each band or artist was plagued by mental health or addiction problems. Maybe this was just rock 'n' roll. Maybe it was a coincidence. Whatever the case, it made total sense as to why she felt so connected to it. It also explained why I did too.

One crisp morning, I found myself walking along the lake shore, feeling worse than ever.

I thought to myself, *How long will this hell last?* Years? Did I fuck up my brain permanently? Was I completely hopeless? As I took in several deep breaths of fresh morning air, I noticed what I at first thought was a rare piece of litter on the beach. I went over and realized my pill bottle had washed up on the shore. I picked it up and felt immediately compelled to open it and down every single pill at once.

Squeezing the bottle, I felt ashamed and angry that it had so much power over me. With just one gulp, I could feel normal again, at least for a few hours. I needed a break from the pain and felt completely willing to give in, telling myself it would be one last time.

I then heard a voice.

"I get it."

It was mom. Startled, I spun around, hiding the pills behind my back. But I knew she saw what I had.

"I want to give up too," she said. "I'd give anything to feel normal again."

She looked cold, standing there shivering with arms crossed. "When did you last feel normal?" I asked.

After pausing to think, she said, "Seems like forever." A loon cried.

"This really hurts," I said, clutching my pills.

"I screwed up everything, Sheena," she said, watching the loon glide along the water and land on its surface, "but it's great knowing I didn't screw up you. How that happened, I don't know."

I didn't know what to say. There was no denying that her life was screwed up, but it seemed pretty clear that mine was as well.

"I feel pretty screwed up, Mom," I said.

She looked at me with sad eyes; she shook her head. "No, you're gonna get past this."

"Yeah?" I said, skeptically.

"I wasn't a good mother. Fuck, I wasn't a mother at all," she said.

I opened the pill bottle and looked inside at the little pile and fantasized about them soothing my brain, going down my throat, into my stomach, and dissolving magic into my bloodstream.

"There's still time," I said as I poured every last pill into my open palm.

Mom watched. I wondered if she was going to stop me or say anything. I wanted her to slap them out of my hand and scold me for being an idiot. But I didn't give her a chance.

Instead, I tossed them into the lake.

Chapter Seventeen

The next morning, not long after mom fell asleep, I found myself sitting on the edge of the bed, shivering in a wrapped blanket, listening to a Chet Baker record while feeling my worst withdrawals yet. It got so bad that I even ran outside and vomited all over the ground. With my head pounding, I wondered how long I would feel this way, or if I caused permanent damage to the part of my brain that felt joy.

Maybe it would come and go. Maybe this is how addicts always felt and why they always went to meetings and said prayers until they inevitably relapsed. My anxieties always led me back to thinking about more pills. Maybe just a few would be okay…just to level me out. I could always wean myself off again, right? Why did I throw those pills away? I just needed to feel a little better to get by. I'd even take ten percent better. Feeling like *this* from now on was not going to work.

As I paced the cabin—wanting nothing more than to black out, to be unconscious—I thought seriously about leaving, driving back to town to score pills, just a few, maybe three or four. Enough to take the edge off. I could easily send a text to my guy back home and be there and back in just a couple of hours, perhaps even before mom was out of bed. She'd never know.

And it wouldn't be a relapse, right? Everything in me wanted to do it. But something—not sure what—stopped me. Minute by minute, I endured the hell, clenching, shaking. Even crying. Mid-morning, I went to check on mom, not having heard a sound from her room for hours. The silence made me a little nervous. The floorboards creaked under my bare feet as I crept toward the closed door and gently pushed it open. To my horror, she wasn't there. I looked around the room like in a game of hide and seek but there was nowhere to hide. She was gone.

I ran outside, around the cabin then down near the water, but still, there was no sign of her anywhere. At a loss, I stared blankly, terrified this could only mean bad things, like being lost in the woods or floating in the lake. Frantic, I ran past the other cabins, eventually finding myself down the road looking everywhere, hoping that she simply went for a walk or a smoke.

But it was as though she vanished into the mist, and after twenty minutes, I feared the worst.

I tried calling her phone knowing she wouldn't answer, and of course, she didn't. I then noticed a new text…from her. I took a deep breath, my hand shook as I tapped my phone.

It said:

'Sheena, I can't do this right now. not ready. 2 much pain. I got a ride but will find you when the time is good. Not now tho. wll get you that money for school. Promise'.

At that moment, I hated her. Really hated her. I crouched down and screamed into my folded arms. It was anger; it was sadness; it was everything. What was I doing all of this for? Why was I such an idiot? I actually had the idea in my head that this was all going to work out. I came for money, but I was coming home with a mother—at least that's what I thought. Now, after days of torment—the soul-tearing withdrawals—she was just going to throw it all away like this? Throw *us* away? Just like that?

No…fuck, no.

When I calmed down slightly, I looked and noticed her text was sent just fifteen minutes old. Thinking she couldn't have been far, I jumped in my car and raced down the road toward town. I wasn't going to let this happen without her facing me one last time. Not again. If she didn't want me, fine, whatever. I'll deal like I've always dealt with it. But I wasn't going to let her turn away again unless I was there in front of her. She wasn't allowed to go away without me watching.

I drove like an insane person, practically veering off the windy road at every bend, as it twisted through the woods and around the lake. I wasn't exactly sure where I was going, but I was fully prepared to go back to that shitty trailer if I had to and walk right up to their door, even if it meant facing Jim. Somehow, I just knew she was going back to him. But why?

It's an eternal mystery. Why do some women go back to the same losers who abuse and make them feel like less than nothing? I guess, with mom, the answer was simple—drugs. Jim could do anything he wanted to her as long as he fed her addiction. It seems I was nothing compared to the power he had over her. Still, I drove.

After twenty minutes, as I was about to pass a gas station, I noticed by sheer chance Jim's hideous yellow car at one of the pumps. By instinct, I made an illegal U-turn and pulled in slowly, keeping my distance. I parked next to a dumpster and saw that mom was definitely in that car. I also saw Jim in the store, waiting in line.

So what now? I thought. Do I drive by and give her the finger and drive off forever? Do I beg her to come back with me? What was I doing there? Did I even want to look at her?

Placing my foot lightly on the gas, I crept my car up next to her. She didn't notice me at first; she seemed to be daydreaming, or maybe she was high already. After a minute, she finally turned toward me but it didn't seem to register at first. She had a vacant look. But when it finally dawned on her that she was caught red-handed, she looked ashamed. And for some weird reason, I felt ashamed too.

I felt like a desperate loser who wouldn't let go of something that should have been let go long before. Still, I wasn't going to say or do anything until she did. I just stared at her like a poker player waiting for the opponent's next move.

She turned away like she wanted to cry. I wanted to cry, too. I wanted her to see my hurt right there in front of her, but she could barely look at me. I stared right into her face as she kept looking into the gas station window at the creep as he approached the cash register. Finally, she rolled down her window.

"Why do you bother with me?" She said.

It was a great question, and I had no answer. "I wish I knew," I said.

"You're better off without me," she said.

This sounded like a bullshit copout. "Right, because being completely alone is really working out for me!"

Mom again looked into the gas station as the loser was placing his items on the counter. She then slumped down into her seat like she wanted to melt into it. She was conflicted, far more conflicted than I wanted her to be. She was torn between her daughter and a drug dealer. Was this going to be the last image I'd have of mom, an image of her covering her face in shame, turning her kid away for the last time?

And it would certainly be the last time because there was no going back once I left that parking lot. Never again would I put myself through it. I'd go back to not giving a shit and coming to terms that I'd one day learn about her inevitable fatal overdose.

As I was about to peel out of the parking lot, mom did the unthinkable; just as Jim was about to exit the store, she jumped out of the yellow car and into mine.

"Go!" She screamed, banging the top of my dash, so I floored it, almost hitting a minivan as it was backing out of a spot. As I hauled ass out of there, I saw Jim in my rear-view mirror, holding a bag of chips and a six-pack, watching us drive off. I couldn't help but laugh as we raced up the road toward the edge of town.

Neither of us said a thing at first. It wasn't a comfortable situation and I'm sure she was as embarrassed as I was pissed. I finally spoke up.

"Is this how it's gonna be now?" I asked.

Like a child caught red-handed, mom was withdrawn, silently staring out the window at the trees going by while scratching the shit out of her arms. She shrugged and said, "Not if I can help it."

"I hope you can help it," I said, thinking hope was all we had.

Chapter Eighteen

A few minutes down the road, we turned into the Graham Lake campground to get our stuff, realizing that Jim's could be close behind. In no time, we were back on the road, both of us really quiet as we drove south with no particular destination or purpose, other than getting away from everything. Perhaps we were scared—I know *I* was—unsure of what the future had in store for us. A million outcomes were playing out in my mind now.

Some were tragic, some were fairy tales. Whatever weird thing mom and I had, this crazy version of a mother-daughter relationship, I wondered if it had a future.

I wasn't sure, but mom was probably just as scared as I was, maybe even more—scared of relapsing at any moment, scared that Jim would go to the ends of the earth to track her down, scared of being a mom again. I knew I was scared of her *not* being a mom again, and that this childhood emptiness never really went away. It had always been deep within me.

After a ten-mile stretch of silence, mom cleared her throat. "How's your grandmother?" She asked with some bitterness in her voice.

"How much do you know?" I asked.

"I know she's sick." I nodded.

For the next few miles, she was silent again, occasionally shaking her head, clearly conflicted. "I guess I should see her," she finally said. "I probably should, right?"

"If you want to," I said.

"It's like Alzheimer's or something?" She asked me.

"Yeah, I guess," I said.

"So her mind's going?"

"Something like that."

"Maybe it's a good thing, if I'm erased in her head," she said.

"That's dumb," I said.

Mom didn't respond because she knew I was right—she just stared out of the window at nothing in particular. Somehow, I could sense her inner struggle as her better nature wanted to see grandma, but the part of her that was poisoned wanted no part of it.

"So…you wanna see grandma or not?" I asked.

After a slight pause, she said, "I don't know, but let's head there in case." And with that, we finally had somewhere to go.

"Might as well," I said.

Soon enough, we were back in New Hampshire. As we made our way over the bridge, I kept wondering why mom and grandma stopped talking. Was it simply the drugs? Or was her addiction a symptom of another problem? I kept wondering why mom wanted to get high in the first place. Was addiction a family curse thing?

I knew a little about grandma's own demons and how the sweet old lady I knew was a drunk before I was born when she was younger and not so sweet. Maybe more is predetermined than we think.

The minute we arrived back in Salem, mom perked up and took in all the familiar sights of her home town.

"What the hell is that?" She said, pointing out the window at the high school as we sat at a stoplight.

"That's Dante's Inferno," I said. "You've been there. You should know."

"What happened to it?"

"Lots of renovations," I said. "They ripped down most of it and added stuff. A new auditorium, actually."

"Looks like a mall now," she said.

I then realized how much had changed since mom had lived in town. One by one, old familiar stores, restaurants and shops were replaced with newer, shinier ones. All the ma and pa stores were driven out of business by all the chain stores that took over the commercial district.

By now, her own home town must have been unrecognizable to her.

"Pull in," she demanded.

"What? Where?" I was confused.

"The school. I wanna see something," she said with no more detail than that. Obeying, I cut over and entered the high school parking lot which was half-filled with trucks and construction equipment, piles of rubble, and concrete barriers. I pulled into the principal's spot where we both got out and started toward the building. It was incredibly surreal seeing the old place half demolished.

As we got closer, we saw that a wrecking ball had knocked over a large portion of the auditorium wall and that we were able to see into its dark interior—the rows of all those uncomfortable seats, the old lighting units, the apron of the worn down wooden stage, as stage I once stood upon back when I was a sophomore; for some reason, I signed up for that year's talent show and performed *Creep* by Radiohead. Needless to say, I didn't win.

Mom climbed over a concrete barrier and got closer to the half-torn wall. "My God, do you believe this? This is so crazy," she said in awe, sidestepping over rubble and piles of brick. Feeling like we were in another dimension, I looked around and followed her as she straddled a low section of the wall and trespassed into what was left of the auditorium. Guided by the light of her iPhone, we soon made our way down the dirt-covered middle aisle, taking it all in a vaguely distant memory.

"This is just so bizarre," she said, looking all around. "So many memories here. Can't believe it's been twenty-five years. God, I'm old!"

"You miss it?" I asked.

"Some of it," she said. "I miss drama."

Now this surprised me. "You were a drama kid?"

"Kinda, for one year. I liked it while it lasted. I was in that witch play…" *"The Crucible*?" I asked.

"That's it! And a musical…*The Music Man."*

I couldn't help but laugh. "You were in a musical? How punk rock of you!"

"I even danced," she said proudly.

She lit a cigarette and led me toward what was left of the backstage area, brushing past the red curtain that was half pulled down. We found ourselves poking through the prop closet, rummaging through the long-forgotten costumes, props, and dozens of discarded scripts.

"Theater people don't throw stuff away," she said, looking through stacks of old plays. According to mom, the prop closet was where she lost her virginity and where she smoked weed for the first time. I wasn't sure why she told me this and felt they were things I didn't need to know about. Soon we were trying on costumes, just for the hell of it, and acting out scenes from the trashed scripts that were scattered all over the place.

It was all pretty strange, but I guess not so much for a couple of withdrawing nomads just trying to distract themselves from their pain. All along, in the back of our minds—in the back of mine, at least—was the fear of not having a place to stay. If we were desperate enough (and we were close to desperate), there was always the shelter downtown, but maybe we had enough cash between the two of us to get a room at the Cozy Nine motel.

Whatever fears we had waiting for us, whatever pain we were trying to stave off, none of it mattered in that moment, among the rubble and old memories. We were like restless ghosts.

Mom then put on a ratty black wig from a trunk and began reciting a witches' speech from *Macbeth,* overdoing it, and cracking herself up in the process. I grabbed a script and joined in. We then started to riff on *The Crucible*—then blending in lines from *Macbeth*—creating an entirely schitzo, ridiculous mash-up scene. We even brought in a few songs from *Grease,* making it all work somehow in a manic fit of pent-up energy.

As it grew dark outside, we quieted down, finishing up with a straight reading from *Death of a Salesman*—mom was Willy Loman, I was Biff. At the end of the hotel scene, mom got quiet.

"Alright, fine. You win," she said.

"What are you talking about?" I asked.

"Let's go see her."

I knew she was talking about grandma, but I didn't know why she thought this was a case of me 'winning'.

"It can't hurt," I said.

"It sure as hell can," she said.

"I guess," said.

I looked past the opening in the wall, into the darkening sky. "Looks like we'll be sleeping in the car," I said.

"Wouldn't be the first time, would it?" She said, referring to the several times we were evicted from apartments or wherever. "We could always sleep in here," she said. "How often do you get to spend the night in the ruins of an old theater?"

"True," I said.

After a few cigarettes and walks around the football field, we grabbed a few worn-out blankets and spread them upon the part of the curtain that was piled on the side of the stage. We spent another hour or two talking about music, life, and how much it all hurt, how much our bodies ached. Then mom got quiet and drifted off to sleep. I could hear her shaking, her trembling breaths as she endured her pain. And, the stiller I got, the more I felt my own agony; and not long after, I, too, fell asleep.

Chapter Nineteen

By the time I was eleven, it became clear to me that I was going to lose her. She was nearly gone already, constantly passed out in her room or out all night with people I didn't know. I wasn't sure when it was going to happen, but I feared it could be at any moment. I feared that one night, she wouldn't come home, or that one morning, she wouldn't wake up. This dread became a part of me, a default setting that has never left my head.

Still, I did everything I could to hang on to her, to make her stay, to love her when she clearly didn't love herself. I cleaned the apartment, made dinner for us as best as I could (usually mac and cheese or pasta), trying not to make her mad at me. But none of it worked. In fact, she kept getting worse. She was on the edge of a rocky cliff, and at any point, her foot was going to slip and I'd lose her forever.

By that spring, my anxiety became unbearable. I had a vague idea of alcohol and why people drank it and why some people drank a lot of it. In movies and on TV shows, it made people laugh and look happy. People partied with it; people turned to it when they were sad and alone. I knew it wasn't it was sort of a bad thing, but people used it anyway, so it must work on some level. And I knew mom drank it on most nights, and I knew where she kept it. And I knew why I wanted to try it.

One night, while I waited for mom to come home, I stood on a chair and took down one of the bottles she kept on top of the fridge. It was a dark bottle with a cork in it, half-filled with something red. Even then, I knew it was wine and that it might help take away what was making me afraid; I knew enough of it could numb me. The smell hit me as I pulled out the loose cork, and it didn't smell like something I wanted to drink—it smelled more like vinegar.

It was a taste for adults, not kids. But I didn't care. I didn't want it for the taste. I poured some into a plastic cup and sat down at our small kitchen table. The stove clock said 8:07 pm which really meant 9:07 pm (mom never changed it for daylight savings), which was far from the time she usually came home, so I was safe from getting caught in the act. After the first careful sip, I felt it burning my throat, so I forced the next one down more quickly, doing my best to ignore the taste.

By the third and fourth sips, I was getting a bit used to it. Right away, I felt it take over. There was a gentle lightness to it, a tingle in my head. I kind of liked it, so I poured another. This time, I downed it in two gulps and liked it more. Whatever this red juice was doing to me, I was okay with it.

For the next few minutes, I sat and stared at nothing in particular. I felt less fixed on my thinking, my worries. Instead, thoughts were flowing through me, and I didn't care what they were. More must have been better, so I took another sip and felt myself not caring about anything. Minutes later, I fell asleep with my head on the table.

I woke up and looked at the clock. 10:27 pm, or rather 11:27 pm. Mom still wasn't home and I knew it would be hours before she would be stumbling through the door then dragging herself to bed. I rammed the cork back into the noticeably emptier bottle, stood up on a chair, and put it back where it was, next to the cereal. Grasping the freezer handle with one hand, I nearly kept myself from tumbling over; I still felt numb but not as happy as before. My worries were there, a bit below the surface for now, but still there, waiting for me.

Cautiously, I stepped off the chair and went into the living room, unsure if I wanted to go to bed or stare at the TV. It was then I heard an ambulance soar past our apartment. This happened almost every night, often waking me out of an already nervous sleep. But for some reason, on this night, I was convinced this one was for mom, that *this* was the one that brought her to the hospital for the last time.

In a panic, I bolted to the window and watched the ambulance blow through the intersection at the corner, splashing red light on all the surrounding tenements and parked cars. I felt helpless, impulsive, like I needed to chase after it all the way to the hospital. Sitting down on the couch, I somehow convinced myself she was okay, or at least alive, that the odds of this ambulance being for her were really low.

But the more I thought about it, the more deeply I breathed, the more I realized that someday—and it was likely very soon— one would certainly have her name on it, and that it was only a matter of time. It seems my existence wasn't enough to make her stop hurting herself and hurting me…hurting us. Was it possible she couldn't see it? Did she not know how scared I was every time she left the apartment, not knowing if I would see her again?

Maybe she was that clueless or maybe I was too silent. Somehow, I had to tell her. If she really knew how I felt, this would all stop. Convinced I was right, I went to my room and pulled my notebook out of my schoolbag. I found a pencil and sat down on my bed. What I had to say was going to be in writing, and the words I would choose were going to be exact, and she would see how I felt.

I sat there staring at the blank page, with so much to say—maybe too much—the pencil hovered an inch over the first line. Then, it all poured over…

Mom,

I'm afraid. All the time I'm afraid and very very sad too. I'm very afraid of losing you and being alone forever. You don't want me to be alone, do you? You are so sick every day and you hardly even look at me. A mom should look at her daughter, right? A mom should do a lot of other things too but I'm okay with just a couple of things. I used to be mad but I know something is wrong with you. Something you can't help yourself with.

I know more than you think I know. I know you are taking stuff that's not medicine like you used to tell me. That was a lie but I'm still not that mad. I kinda know what that stuff is and it's not good for you at all. It makes you like a zombie and you could die from it. Did you know you could die from it? Well, you know now, okay?

Like I said I'm afraid. Because I don't want to be alone in the world, so I'm writing this so you'll promise to stop. My birthday is in three weeks and that's what I want…for you to stop.
Will you do it? Say yes okay?

Love,
Sheena

I put down the pencil and read my letter at least ten times. At first, I was convinced she'd read it and immediately change paths, but the more I thought about it, the more I doubted it. Why would a dumb letter change anything? This is how it was and how it would always be. Nothing changes.

Some girls have mothers who care, who bring their daughters to playgrounds and waterparks, and show them how to do makeup and nails. Some girls have moms who stay in bed all day and who leave at night. Some girls have moms who OD.

As I left my room, I could feel my sadness change very quickly to rage. I wanted to accept things as they were, but for the first time, anger took over me. This letter was already a lie. I *was* mad. As I was about to tear up my letter, I noticed mom's lighters on the coffee table. I only paused a moment before I impulsively picked it up and set fire to my letter. Watching it go up in a small smooth flame was a beautiful, satisfying feeling, but it only lasted a minute before the flame tore into the letter, brushing my hand, and forcing me to let go before I could even take one step toward the sink.

Before I knew it, my dropped letter was burning on top of a pile of mom's laundry, and then the laundry itself was burning. I froze. I had no idea of what to do other than run to the sink for water. By the time I returned with a full cereal bowl, the flames were higher than my waist. The water did almost nothing, so I tried again, then again, and decided that getting out was the only thing to do.

I banged on the doors of the four other apartments as I made my way down the hall and down the stairs. Thankfully, everyone made it out. The fire trucks made it in time to save the building, but our apartment was burned up badly, so we had to move again to a similar tenement down the street. I wish I could say that mom saw this as a cry for help and that this horrible night changed everything, but when she came home later that night and spoke with the fireman, she simply looked at me with a cold lifeless glare. I think it was the first time she looked at me in months.

Chapter Twenty

It had to be a couple of hours later when I woke up to the sounds of sirens and car doors slamming. I sat up and saw two police cars beyond the torn auditorium walls; then, turning around, I saw flames rising up and engulfing much of the torn curtain. Some of the fire had spread to the condemned walls. Two officers ran in and pulled us out into the warm night; one officer had to shout and shake mom to wake her.

As we were led toward a safe distance, groggy and not fully aware of what was going on, a fire truck pulled up and four firefighters got out and immediately went to work. The only explanation I could think of was cigarette butts. As the firefighters sprayed the fire, one officer marched up to us and asked a more than legitimate question: "So what went on here?"

Mom looked too out of it to respond coherently, so I did. "I'm not sure."

"You're not sure?" The officer repeated, who wasn't thrilled about being there in the middle of the night.

"Not really," I said.

"Why were you sleeping in there?" He asked, eyeing my mother.

"Because we were tired," quipped mom. The officer didn't like her answer in the slightest. I noticed him take a deep, methodical breath like he was trying to calm down. After a few minutes, when the fire was under control and practically extinguished, a firefighter emerged from the smoky torn walls, holding up what appeared to be a cigarette butt.

"No surprise here," he said, giving mom and me a look as he handed the butt to the cop.

"Alright, get in," he said, opening the door to his cruiser.

"Are we under arrest or something?" Mom asked, annoyed.

The cop looked more annoyed. "We definitely have a few questions. Let's go."

Mom didn't seem to like the idea. "Whatever…" She huffed and mumbled under her breath while getting into the cruiser. I slipped in beside her.

Thirty minutes later, we were at the station sitting at a table. Mom still seemed out of it. She was compelled to act bitchy when it came to dealing with cops, constantly rolling her eyes and sighing at every request. I was scared but trying to be nice in hopes of getting out of there as soon as possible. After waiting thirty minutes or so, a detective-looking guy entered the room and sat down across from us.

"Time for our interrogation?" Mom asked with a smirk.

"You're not gonna say hello, Veronica?" He said.

Mom's only response was a suspicious look.

"Class of '91, right? Jeff Lindsey? Don't remember me, do you?"

She squinted like it would help her to remember. "Sorry," she said. "I remember almost nothing from high school. Which is probably a good thing."

This guy, realizing cordiality wasn't my mom's strength, placed his hand flat on the table like it was time to get to the point. "Look. There's little doubt that you two started the fire with a cigarette," he said. "This might be a case of accidental arson, you know."

"So does this mean jail?" She asked. "Can you please get to the point?"

The detective paused and looked up from his notes. "Do you two have a place to go? Are you staying anywhere?"

Mom shrugged. "Not sure yet."

He looked down at his notes. "I am seeing here, Sheena, you're at the children's home?"

"No, I'm not there anymore. I left. I'm eighteen," I said.

"Veronica, you have an address in Maine?" he asked.

Mom didn't like all of the questions: "It's legal to take a little road trip to New Hampshire last I checked, right?"

The guy stared her down; to his credit, he kept himself remarkably calm. "Driving to New Hampshire is fine. But trespassing and setting fires isn't."

Mom rolled her eyes.

"There was little damage. It was a demolition zone anyway," the cop said. It seemed like he wanted to give us a break, which I certainly appreciated. Mom, however, refused to make eye contact and seemed quite unmoved.

The detective got up and shoved in his chair. "Let's go," he said.

"Where?" I asked.

"I'll take you back to your car at the school," he said. "But you can't hang around there. You need to find somewhere to go, okay?"

"Thank you," I said.

"We have somewhere to go," mom said.

Chapter Twenty-One

After we were dropped off and got back into the car, mom insisted that we drive all around town and pass all her familiar haunts only to discover most of them were no longer there.

"Are you kidding? They closed the Pour House?" She asked, outraged, as though an old grungy, independent stood a chance in the age of Starbucks. We then drove by an Olive Garden where Ralph's Diner used to be, then past a pharmacy where a record store once stood. Mom got quiet.

After about an hour of driving around town, I realized mom was stalling.

"Can we go see her now?" I finally asked, stopping the car.

Mom closed her eyes and nodded, as though the idea itself was painful. "Yeah, you're right," she said. "You're always right."

This was good enough for me, so I got back on the road and headed to Windermere Assisted Living which was only a few minutes away. Mom's anxiety was obvious: her legs were shaking, her breaths were loud and short. As we got closer, I was sure she was going to make up some excuse to not go in. But, to my amazement, she didn't.

She was lost in thought, probably playing out what she wanted to say in her head. Before I knew it, we were in the rehab parking lot. Mom sat there with her hand on the door handle, frozen.

I took the other hand. "Whatever happens in there, you'll be glad we did this."

"Thanks, Mommy…" she said with a wise-ass smile.

We finally made our way in, signed the guest book, and got on the elevator. I could tell mom was incredibly nervous—she said nothing and had this quizzical look in her eyes, like she was thinking deeply of what she was going to say to grandma. When the elevator door opened, I stepped forward, but mom didn't move.

"You coming?" I asked, looking back.

Mom's darting eyes met mine, and she nodded. "Yeah…okay," she said, walking out of the elevator in a haze. I could see her tremors from ten feet away.

We took our time walking, passing dark silent rooms, passing nurses with blank expressions. No one likes the smell of nursing homes, but to me, the sounds are worse—machines beeping, robotic PA announcements, the occasional moans from dark in-patient rooms. Mom took my hand and squeezed it like she needed some sort of transfer of emotional energy and thought I had some to spare.

When we finally got to the door, it was only half open. Mom paused for a moment then placed her hand flat on the door, taking a deep breath. Then, with a nervous smile, she looked at me and swung it wide open.

The room was dim with shadow, lit only by the faint light from behind the window blinds. But grandma was not there. Both hospital beds were empty and perfectly made. To my surprise, my aunt, Laurie, was seated in the corner chair packing a bag. She looked up at us with wet, red eyes, and she didn't seem all that happy or surprised to see us. By the way she reacted, we could have been anyone.

"Lor?" Mom said, like she barely recognized her own sister.

My aunt stood, and went to my mom. After whispering in her ear and hugging her, I knew she wouldn't act like this unless grandma had died and that we were too late. Mom broke down and cried into Aunt Laurie's shoulder as I watched, knowing that I couldn't join in and be real about it. If anything, I mourned for what grandma and I almost had. So, yeah, I guess I was sad.

Twenty minutes later, we were back in the car following Aunt Laurie back to her house, the house that once belonged to grandma, the house I once considered home or something like it. Aunt Laurie invited us back there for dinner when she learned we had nowhere else to go. Mom kept rubbing off tears and sniffling for the entire ride, not saying much. I wanted to comfort her, to say something meaningful, but nothing came to me.

Dinner was awkward. My uncle, Carl, who rarely spoke, was there shoveling chicken pot pie into his mouth and didn't seem overly thrilled we were there. Mom and Aunt Laurie didn't seem to have much to say to one another, but my aunt was really trying to talk to mom who was in a truly cagey mood.

"Still living in Maine?" Aunt Laurie asked.

"Kinda," mom answered.

"What's that mean, kinda?" Uncle Carl asked taking another spoonful. "Do you or don't you?"

"It's complicated."

Aunt Laurie looked stumped. "What are you doing for work?" She asked.

Mom shrugged. "Let's just say I'm between jobs."

"Oh. Still doing music?"

"Kinda, yeah."

It was super awkward. Mom was clearly jonesing and didn't want to be bothered, which came off as rude; this pissed me off considering my aunt was nice enough to invite us over when I'm sure it was the last thing she wanted. I figured Aunt Laurie knew this came with the territory. I heard somewhere—probably from mom—that they constantly fought growing up. With similar black straight hair, the same brown almond eyes, and normie clothes, my aunt looked like a suburban version of mom.

They were close in age but couldn't be more different. But now they shared a strange cocktail of emotions, dealing with the death of a mother who wasn't exactly Carol Brady.

After another long, uncomfortable pause, Aunt Laurie suddenly blurted out, "Mom wanted to be cremated."

"How do you know?" Mom asked.

"She said so," Aunt Laurie said.

Mom looked up with a mouthful of salad, unsure of what to say. "Yeah, okay…fine," she said. I'm not sure it mattered to her. I could tell she was on edge, trying to stay composed when she wanted to rip off her own skin. She was really feeling the withdrawal now.

"Maybe we should hold a little ceremony or something, too," my aunt said. "Close family only."

"We have close family?" Mom answered.

Ignoring the quip, my aunt turned to me. "So how've you been, Sheena? How was graduation?"

"It was alright," I said, thinking if she cared, she would have come.

"Got any plans?"

"For what?"

"You know, what you'll be doing next."

"I have a few ideas," I said.

"Such as?"

Mom dropped her fork onto the plate. "Is this an interrogation or something?"

My aunt and uncle looked at each other with raised eyebrows, as if to say, *There she goes again*. Mom was looking away toward the wall, shaking and darting her eyes around the room. I just knew it was taking everything for her to not leave.

"Just want to make sure you both are okay," my aunt said. "I didn't mean anything by it."

Mom started scratching her arms. "It would be great if people would start meaning stuff." My aunt, trying to be the bigger person, didn't say anything. She knew her sister well enough to know it was best to take it down a notch whenever possible.

After a long pause, my aunt asked if we had anywhere to go, anywhere to sleep tonight.

Mom didn't notice, but I saw my uncle squirm in his chair and give my aunt the evil eye for going there. I couldn't blame him.

Mom took a slow sip of water. "We'll figure it out," she said, but as she tried to put down her water, the glass slipped out of her weak trembling hand. Water went all over the table.

"Shit!" Mom yelped, covering her face in shame. She was growing more agitated by the second.

"Why not stay here until you figure it out?" Aunt Laurie said while getting paper towels to wipe up the water. My uncle nearly choked on his crescent roll.

And just like that, we were houseguests, residing downstairs on an old pull-out couch in a dim, partially finished basement with wood paneling. It was musty and cold but might as well have been a luxury suite as far as I was concerned. As long as I wasn't sleeping in a car again, I was cool with it. Once we were settled in, exhausted, flat on our backs upon the pull-out couch, we suddenly had time to think about whatever was next.

"I guess I'll go back to the bakery," I said.

"Maybe I'll wait tables again," mom said.

"Is that what you want?" I asked.

"I'm not sure wanting has much to do with it," she said, looking more depressed than I'd ever seen her. At that moment, she was looking at an old picture of grandma that happened to be hanging on the wall across the room.

She tried to hide it, but mom's eyes were wet and she was sniffling, so I held her hand as tenderly as I could.

"I thought there'd be more time to say what I had to say," mom whispered.

"What did you have to say?" I asked.

It looked like mom was really trying to answer this, but it was also like she didn't quite know. "I think I'd start with 'Sorry'."

"Tell her," I said pointing to her picture. "…in your head."

She nodded.

Mom's grief combined with her withdrawal had to be complete hell. She seemed empty of everything except pain. I felt it, too, and wondered how long we were expected to take it without giving in.

Chapter Twenty-Two

After a long, emotional day, no one seemed to have the energy to do anything other than stare blankly at the TV, so we just sat there in the living room, still in our dark funeral clothes, barely talking. I was in the rocking chair in the corner of the room and mom was slumped in the recliner while my aunt was falling asleep on my uncle's lap on the couch. Mom was in rough shape and kept looking at her phone, receiving and responding to a flurry of texts.

This made me completely nervous. There could only be one person texting her this relentlessly at this hour. Her phone kept vibrating on the end table next to her, and of course, she'd pick it up every time to look. Leaning forward, I kept trying to see who it was. Whoever it was would not give it a rest.

My eyes grew heavy as I watched, and soon, I was asleep.

An hour later, mom brushed past me as she got up to use the bathroom and woke me up. My aunt and uncle were fast asleep on the couch and the TV was still on and showing an infomercial. Mom's phone started to vibrate again on the floor next to the recliner. Texts were coming in fast, so I got up slowly, tiptoed across the room, and picked it up, listening for the bathroom door to open.

The phone vibrated in my hand. Then again, then again. I tapped her screen and saw that it was Jim. Most of the texts were short, misspelled ramblings, and I could barely keep up with them as they came in. But they quickly became disturbing:

YOU CAN'T HIDE
I'LL FIND U!
YOU'LL NEVER STOP USING
TXT BACK NOW
I FIND WHERE YOU R

I sat back down, shaking, knowing Jim was crazy enough to chase mom. The worst scenarios were playing out in my mind which included Jim showing up suddenly and taking mom, through force or manipulation. Still, the fact that mom wasn't replying to him was somewhat comforting.

After hearing the bathroom door open, I got up, tossed her phone down, and ran back to my chair. Mom sat, lowered the recliner, and thumbed through her messages while crying herself to sleep. When she was finally snoring, I stood, took a quilted blanket from the arm of the couch, and covered her with it. I then made my way downstairs and laid down on the pull-out bed with a million notions swirling in my head.

Should I go to the police? Should I tell mom what I know and convince her to drive as far as we can? Thinking this made me pissed at myself. Running away was getting old real fast. Why should we keep running from that asshole? Were we going to spend the rest of our lives looking over our shoulders, scared of this piece of shit loser? With grandma dying and everything else that was going on, my head was pounding.

I started fantasizing about pills. Handfuls of pills. I imagined ten jumbo tablets in the palm of my hand and how blissful they would make me feel inside. I lusted at the thought of white magic dust dissolving into my bloodstream. My aunt's medicine cabinet then came to mind and the pills I saw her down before dinner a couple of nights before. I got up, locked myself in the bathroom, opened the mirror, and spotted a bottle of Ativan which, for me, was close enough to Xan.

I uncapped the bottle and stared at the little pile of white capsules, telling myself there was no way she'd notice if I only took a few. And I probably would have if I didn't look up at my reflection in the mirror and notice how much I looked like mom in that moment. Maybe it was the exhaustion or the lighting, or because I was totally worn down, but I looked twenty years older. I looked more like her. After placing the pills carefully back on the shelf and closing the mirror, I climbed into the pull-out bed downstairs.

It was a night of tossing and turning. For hours, I tried to get comfortable so I could fall asleep and escape these impulses, the urge to steal drugs like a junkie. Her sobriety was pretty much tied to mine now. If I gave in, I was sure she would too.

Not long after I finally fell asleep, I woke to the sound of mom's phone vibrating non-stop again through the floor directly above my pull-out bed.

After about the twentieth time, I kicked off the blankets and went upstairs ready to kill someone. I saw that my aunt and uncle went into their bedroom, but mom was still on the recliner, sleeping in a fetal position. Just as I had thought, the phone was on the floor, lighting up and moving around with every vibration, not disturbing mom in the least as she slept.

With the floor creaking under my feet, I moved closer, careful not to bump into any furniture. Each time it lit up, I froze, hoping mom wouldn't wake and catch me. Finally, I knelt, picked up the phone, and saw these were all calls from Jim. I pressed ignore and realized there were twenty missed calls. I was so enraged by this I wanted to smash the phone against the wall or run it over with my car.

I actually wanted to run *Jim* over with my car. I was so pissed that by the time the next call came, I stormed into the next room and answered it, not once asking myself if it was a good idea.

"What do you want, asshole?" I said in a screaming whisper.

I heard nothing in response at first. But I knew he was there, I could tell. Even over the phone, I felt his loathsome presence.

"Who…this Sheena?" It sounded like he was grinning sadistically on the other end, like he wanted it to be me for some twisted reason.

"Leave mom alone," I said, trying to sound tough and probably coming off as scared.

"Did you call her *mom*?" He asked. "You really think she's a mom?"

"I'll call her what I want. It's none of your business."

"You're wasting your time," he said.

"Just leave us alone," I said.

"I'm gonna find you guys," he said. "And she's gonna come back."

"She won't."

"You watch. You think she's kicked her habit?"

I didn't respond because I really didn't know the answer.

"I have what she really wants, and you know that. Don't you?" He said.

Again, I had no real answer, so I just listened to the dead air.

Then, I could hear the grin on his face when he said, "I have what you want, too." I hung up on him and went back into the living room, silently placed the phone on the end table near mom. At this point, there was nothing else to do but go to bed and try to forget for a while. I wanted to forget Jim, mom's issues, drugs, me not going to college in the fall. I wanted to forget everything. I wanted to erase my mind.

The next day, I drove to the bakery to see if Mr. Marquis would give me back some hours, which he gladly did being so short of help, and just like that, I was back to work that night and was scheduled almost every day that week. Though my withdrawal symptoms were constant, I still felt slightly normal being in a familiar place with familiar faces who all seemed genuinely happy to see me back. Mom, though, spent most days hanging around my aunt's house, lying in bed.

When she left our room for dinner or to watch TV, it was obvious she was still in a lot of pain. I was nervous that mom's condition wasn't really improving. She was still shaking, still moody as hell. Then I thought: Why would it be any different? For most of her adult life, mom had chemicals injected into her veins on a daily basis. It's always been a part of her. To suddenly not feel something so familiar inside her must've been total hell.

Not feeding my addiction was pure hell, but it was getting easier to live with by the day. For mom, this was probably only the start of the torture, and I was nervous about how long she would be able to bear it. I always made sure to check her phone as she slept; thankfully, calls and texts from Jim weren't coming in as much now, which also made me nervous for some reason.

I got up one morning at 4 am to help make bread. When I arrived at the bakery, as usual, I was put in charge of the kneading, which I once found boring but now felt therapeutic. It gave me a chance to think about stuff or not think at all if I didn't feel like it. That morning, I had two things on my mind: mom (of course) and college. Now that I was in some kind of routine, I figured it wouldn't hurt to stop by the community college to see if I had any options at all, even though it was August now with the semester starting within weeks.

As I patted the dough with flour and pressed on it, I found myself daydreaming, picturing myself in class, taking notes. It felt right being there, even in my imagination. The idea of chasing a goal, having a purpose—it felt incredible, felt real. But at the moment, it also felt like nothing more than a fantasy.

Later on that morning, I was behind the shop taking a cigarette break when Carl poked his head out of the back door and said I had a phone call. This never happened, so I knew it couldn't have been good.

I picked up the cordless phone. "Hello?"

"Sheena?" It was my aunt who sounded pretty upset.

"Yeah."

"We're in the ER with your mom, but she's okay, don't worry…"

"What are you talking about?" I asked.

"Apparently, she hitch-hiked here and told the nurses she's having severe back issues." I didn't respond immediately. I just tried to let what she said make sense somehow but it wasn't happening.

I said, "She's never said anything about back issues to me."

My aunt got quiet for a moment, then said, "Sheena, I know the ER doctor a little. He told me their database shows your mother has a history of trying to get pills from a number of hospitals. Do you think this is what happened tonight?"

My long exhale must've sounded like a gust of wind on the other end of the phone. "I guess so," I said.

I rushed home on my lunch break to see that mom was predictably in bed. Through the dim, musty basement air, I saw her lying there on top of the covers in a t-shirt and jeans, earbuds in her ears. I sat down at the foot of the bed and saw that her eyes were open, staring at the wood panel wall. I was in no mood to be warm, so with my arms crossed, I waited for her to say something.

"This is hard, girl," she said, finally.

"What is?" I asked.

"I don't know. Life."

"You're telling me?"

My rhetorical question must've hit her between the eyes because she started crying. She pulled a pillow over her face and let it all out, whimpering into the bedspread.

"This is Hell, Sheena," she said, her voice muffled. "I'm in Hell every day."

"I know you are, Mom," was all I could think to say. I had nothing. I suppose I could have said something like, 'Let's get you help' or 'You gotta keep fighting', but acknowledging her pain was the only thing that made sense in that moment, realizing that her pain made it impossible for her to acknowledge mine.

And I wish I could say this was the last incident. It was only a few days later when I woke up in the middle of the night to the sound of smoke detectors going off. Sitting up, I smelled smoke and heard a commotion upstairs. Mom was not with me, so I jumped up and ran upstairs and saw the entire kitchen engulfed in smoke. My aunt was standing there helplessly as my uncle opened the oven and blasted the inside of it with a small fire extinguisher.

"What happened? Where's Mom?" I shouted.

My aunt looked at me and said nothing; she was in a complete stupor, and I could tell she knew mom was high. After opening the kitchen windows, the smoke cleared, we saw mom sleeping in the recliner, completely unaware that the house had almost burned down. I went over and shook her. She looked at me in a complete daze, with an expression that didn't seem to recognize her own daughter.

A couple of minutes later, my uncle pulled a charred pizza out of the oven that mom apparently forgot about. It seemed she thought it was a good idea to eat pizza in the middle of the night and to cook it while still in the box. This was when I knew that mom was getting high again. There was no doubt, and for the next few days, I refused to speak to her—to even look at her.

Chapter Twenty-Three

A few nights later, mom had enough of my silent treatment. I tossed my dirty clothes on the floor next to my bag and plugged the charger into my phone. Mom was on the floor butchering *Redemption Song* on the guitar, strumming like she just learned to play the week before. Frustrated, she stopped.

"Shit…what's the goddamn chord here?" I knew she wanted my attention.

"No clue," I said, making it obvious I was still pissed at her for being an idiot when we've come this far.

Mom ignored my passive-aggressive comment and continued playing as I made a big point of putting earbuds into my ears. She kept strumming, harder and harder. I turned up my music and drowned her out, but I could tell she was mad and was taking it out on the guitar with her violent strumming. She only stopped when one of the strings broke. She tossed the guitar aside and folded her arms. I knew she was waiting for me to say something but I didn't. I wanted her to squirm.

"So you're mad at me now?" I could hear her say, finally, through the intro to *Waiting For You* by Nick Cave.

Taking out one earbud, I pretended not to hear her. "Huh?"

"You're pissed at me, right? It's obvious," she said, not making eye contact.

"It should be obvious," I said. "There's a lot to be pissed about."

Mom stammered. She wasn't high at that moment but she was definitely feeling the effects of her last fix. I wanted to say something meaningful, something that would grab her soul by the hair so she'd stop going. But there were no words. No matter what I said or how loud I said it, mom was thinking about her next high. I felt ridiculous believing that there'd always be room for me inside her fevered brain. All my life she chose the needle over me; why would she change now?

"Are you gonna tell me?" Mom asked.

"Tell you what?"

"Why are you giving me an attitude?"

I laughed a little, laid down, and turned away from her.

"So that's it?" She said. "No explanation."

"Just let me go to sleep," I said.

Mom stood up and came to the foot of the bed. "You're gonna ignore me now? This is what we're doing?" She said.

"You know," I said.

"Know what?" She asked.

I paused with Nick Cave in mid-croon but didn't say anything. She had to know what I was pissed and hurt about. It's always the same thing.

Mom sat on the bed. "I'm fine, Sheena," she said. "I know what you're thinking. It's not that."

Again, even now, the lies? I sat up and shot her a look that could only read as disbelief.

"Oh, yeah?" I said. "Prove it."

She immediately got defensive. "Whatever—then don't believe me."

"Give me your bag," I demanded.

"My bag? Why?"

"You know why."

At that moment, I saw myself as a kid again, finding the bad needle inside mom's bag as everything dumped onto the floor. After everything we've been through and for most of my life, there were drugs in her bag. Why would this change?

"Fine," she said as she went toward the other side of her bed where her bag was; she only made it halfway before hesitating. She wasn't about to hand me her bag because we both knew what was inside it. I lurched up and reached for it.

"Don't...Sheena!" Mom said, running over. We both took hold of the bag at the same time and were quickly pulling at it. In one furious tug, I ripped the open bag out of her hands, sending everything inside it everywhere. A giant pill bottle dropped onto the bed in front of us. I wasn't surprised in the slightest but it still killed me to see them.

Mom lowered her head like a child caught stealing candy as I picked up one the bottle and saw they were prescribed to someone else, someone named Stephen Rice. Again, not surprised.

"I don't know what to say to you, kiddo," she said, and that's all she said that night. I threw the pill bottle at her, hitting her in the arm, and laid down facing the other direction. I had nothing more to give her. After a minute of just standing there, she went slowly up the stairs. Where she went after that, I had no idea where she went, but I heard the front door of the house open and close, and I heard her pick up her pills.

Maybe I should just give up, too, I thought; maybe I should just get my own bottle of stolen pills. Maybe that's where I'm headed anyhow, so why avoid it any longer?

Chapter Twenty-Four

I slept through the morning and well into the afternoon, missing my shift at work and only waking when my phone started to vibrate on the end table. It was my boss wondering where the hell I was. After I apologized a thousand times—giving myself a fifty percent shot of getting fired—he told me to come in and help with a huge cupcake order for a kid's birthday party. As I showered and got dressed, I noticed no sign of mom. Wherever she went, she was there all night, and I did my best to not care. If she didn't give a shit, why should I?

Still, I couldn't help wondering if she was out there somewhere, scavenging for pills with some lowlife, or worse, headed right back to her Maine trailer like none of this ever happened.

The more I tried not to think about her, the more she filled my brain. The whole time my boss kept getting on me about the shitty job I was doing with frosting the cupcakes, making corrections each time he checked on me. And he was right, my work was complete shit, but I just couldn't bring myself to care about unicorn cupcakes when my mother could be lying dead in a gutter.

So later on when some lady came to pick up her order of glittery pink cupcakes for her little princess, I really wasn't in the right headspace to deal with her and all her complaints.

"These don't look right," she said, after opening the box.

"What do you mean?" I asked as she examined each cupcake.

"They don't look like unicorns at all."

"That's because they're cupcakes," I said, knowing I messed up a little on the ears making them look more like bunnies. But I wasn't going to admit it to this soccer mom. They weren't perfect, but they were fine.

She didn't appreciate my answer at all. "Excuse me? Want to try that again?"

I knew I wasn't providing the best customer service but I just wasn't in the mood. "No," I said, smirking.

"No?" She seemed like a woman who was used to getting her way.

"No," I repeated.

"Get your manager," she demanded. "I'm not paying for these."

"There's nothing wrong with them," I insisted.

"Get your manager!" She repeated, loudly.

"Don't yell at me."

"Did you make these monstrosities?" She asked.

"Maybe." I've dealt with customers like her before; the ones who drive up in a Porsche that will haggle the shit out of people to save a buck. I wasn't about to put up with her normie shit. Not that day.

My boss must've heard the commotion because he came out and immediately tried to deescalate the situation. When he saw how mad the woman was, he apologized and told her there was no charge. Carl was always too nice—which explained why I was still employed. As he offered to bring the free cupcakes out to her car, I butted in and insisted on doing it myself.

Carl looked nervous as I took the large box from him and followed the woman out the door and to her white convertible. And it turns out, he had every right to be nervous, because when I saw the sticker on her car that said *Penn State Mom*, I completely lost it.

In my own defense, she was a complete bitch to me, even *after* Carl waived the charge. She opened the door and pointed at the backseat like she was some queen and I was her little servant. It might have been her smirk that put me over the edge. With total *I-don't-care-anymore* abandonment, with my hands shaking from having no Xanax in my blood, I threw the box of cupcakes into the back seat. As soon as it made an impact, the cupcakes tumbled out onto the backseat, smearing pink, purple and blue frosting everywhere.

The whole thing felt like it was out of body and happening in slow motion. Kind of shocked and kind of gleeful, I slapped my hand over my mouth. The woman was also in shock, but before she could say or do anything about it, I sprinted off, jumped in my car, and drove away laughing. On my way back to my aunt's, I pretty much figured I was out of a job.

Carl was a pushover and had always put up with my less than dependable work ethic, but even he wasn't going to let this one slide. I silenced my phone because I knew within minutes he'd be calling.

When I got to the house, my heart dropped when I still saw no sign of mom and discovered that her bag and guitar were gone. Shaking, I went outside to the back porch and saw my aunt sitting in her chair with tears running down her cheek. I didn't want to know. I didn't want to ask. But I knew I was about to get bad news. I only hoped it wasn't the bad news I always figured one day would come. The permanent kind.

I opened the screen door and just stood there and tried to numb my feelings for what I was about to be told. "She's gone," my aunt told me.

"Where?"

"She didn't say. I tried to talk to her but she was completely out of it. It's like she didn't even know me. She mumbled something and got into someone's car."

I shook my head. But why did I expect anything different? My aunt got up and hugged me, which was weird but still felt good. I hugged her back, unable to hold back my own tears.

"Your mom does care about you, Sheena," she said. "She's just not in control of…"

"Anything," I said, finishing her sentence. I took out my phone and tried calling her, but it kept going directly to voicemail. Then something occurred to me.

"The car that picked her up? What kind was it?" I asked.

My aunt thought about it for a minute. "I'm not sure," she said. "But I think it was kind of junky…and black, I think."

"And you didn't stop her?" I asked.

My aunt looked me dead in the eyes. "Sheena, I've tried to stop your mother countless times."

I didn't want to believe it, but it was safe to assume she had gone off with Jim. It all seemed inevitable. My aunt's eyes turned sad but she didn't really know what to say. I knew she felt horrible for me, a girl whose mother always leaves.

Chapter Twenty-Five

It was impossible to know exactly when mom would disappear, but I knew it was always going to happen eventually. She disappeared regularly throughout my childhood—sometimes for a couple hours, other times, for several weeks or even months. Who knows where she went and who she went with. But I learned to sense when it was coming, and I learned to live with the fear of her leaving, even during the stretches when she played the mom role fairly convincingly by taking me to soccer or having coffee with other normie moms during playdates with normie friends.

But beneath it all, anxiety pulsated within me constantly, like a demon; it was a dread that I never got used to, something I had to live with, this fear could up and leave at any moment.

Whenever she'd return, I knew it was only a matter of time before she'd do it again. And she always came back…except the last time when she left for good.

It happened at the end of one of mom's normie phases, and this time, she was really trying. She'd get me up in the morning for school, cook breakfast, even tell me to do my homework at night. Mom even went to an open house once that year looking like a soccer mom with her short parted hair and bright sweater. It was weird, but I was happy she seemed into the mother thing, so I decided to enjoy it while it lasted.

I was particularly happy that she was willing to pick me up after choral an hour after school, three days a week. And on May afternoons, she was very nearly on time.

But during the week of my thirteenth birthday, our make-believe fantasy world came crashing down. By now, I was an expert on mom's mood swings, and I knew something was wrong on our way to the park where mom had arranged to have a little picnic lunch to celebrate my birthday with a couple of friends and their mothers. She almost went off the road a couple of times and seemed totally out of it. She wasn't talking much, and whenever she did say something, it was negative and pissy.

"Shit," she said, as we pulled into the park.

"What?" I asked.

"Forgot plastic forks."

"That's okay."

"No, it's not okay. What are they going to eat cake with?"

"You can eat cake with your hands."

"Why do I fuckin' bother?"

The soccer mom version of mom was nowhere to be found. She put the car in park and slouched in her seat like forgetting forks was the end of the world. In fact, it looked like she wanted to cry. Whenever she got into these moods, the smallest thing would seem like a world ending catastrophe in her head. After a couple of minutes of pouting in silence, we got out of the car and claimed a picnic table between the playground and the woods.

Mom, who at times seemed to forget my age, covered them with a pink girly plastic table cloth with cupcake designs all over it. She then put out bags of chips, soda, and placed my pink and purple musical birthday cake at the center. Soon, Jocelyn arrived with her mom, then not long after that, Gabby arrived with hers. At first, no one was talking much and it felt a little awkward; I mean, they were my friends, I guess, but I didn't know them too well because I was new to the district after moving again.

But mom pressed me two weeks before to pick who I wanted to invite. Jocelyn and Gabby were the girls I knew the best from after school chorus so here they were.

The three of us ended up at a different picnic table while our moms talked about whatever moms talked about. Gabby and Jocelyn were on their phones, ignoring everything while I just sort of sat there with nothing to do.

Finally, I tried to make small talk. "You guys psyched for the concert?" Later on that week was the end of the year concert which was kind of a big deal for chorus and band kids.

Gabby shrugged, eyes glued to her phone. Jocelyn said, "Sure, I guess."

"I think the altos are flat a lot," I said, "but I think we sound good."

Neither girl seemed to have the slightest opinion on the matter but they did start rating the boys in chorus. There weren't many of them, but Gabby and Jocelyn began declaring who the 'kissable' ones were. This time, I was the one with no opinion. My attention drifted to mom over at the party table. Things over there also seemed forced.

Mom didn't seem to be saying anything to the other mothers who seemed to know each other well enough. With sunglasses on, head propped up by her hand, mom was not herself—at least not the version I wanted. She was sort of acting like the mom who doesn't care. The mom who passes out in random places. The mom who leaves.

Suddenly, Jocelyn and Gabby went over to their moms and asked if they could go walk down near the pond. When we all got permission, we went down to the embankment where a dad was fishing with his little kid. With a smirk, Gabby opened her mini backpack and pulled out a small bottle of clear liquid.

"Check it out," she said, proudly.

"Where did you get that?" Jocelyn asked.

"I got my sources," Gabby said.

"What is?" Jocelyn asked.

"Vodka," Gabby declared proudly.

Very little shocked me at this point in my life, but this certainly did. In chorus class, Gabby and Jocelyn were angels. They got driven around in mini vans and probably went apple picking in the fall. But now it seemed like they were also developing a booze habit at a very young age, preparing to be bored ex-wives one day.

"Let's go," Gabby said, making her way across a short wooden bridge that crossed over the lake and led to a wooded path.

Following Gabby's lead, we all started running deeper and deeper into the woods until we were out of the sights of our mothers, who weren't paying much attention to us anyhow. With the exception of a few hikers here and there, the path was nearly empty as we made our way around the lake. Finally, we followed Gabby behind a large tree by the edge of the lake. After glancing around, she took out the bottle and took a swig, practically choking in the process.

She passed it to Jocelyn—who also gagged on it—then it came to me. This wasn't the first time I tried alcohol; mom once let me take a sip of her beer one night when friends were over. It tasted gross, but this was even worse.

"We're dead if we get caught," Jocelyn said.

Gabby took another swig. "Let's not get caught then."

A few more sips and a couple of minutes later, we were doing our very best to get caught—we were obnoxiously loud, singing songs from chorus class, throwing sticks and rocks into the lake. Not long after, Gabby hurled a stick at a family of ducks. She laughed and tossed a few more, nearly hitting one. Jocelyn then joined in.

This pissed me off, so I yelled, "What the hell are you doing?" The vodka made me completely fearless, so I shoved Gabby. Jocelyn stared at us, not quite sure of what to do. Gabby seemed a bit in shock, too, at my outburst that probably seemed to come out of nowhere.

Gabby pushed me back, hard, and I fell backward and part of me nearly landed in the water. "What's wrong with you?" She shouted back.

I got back up, slowly, then charged at her, knocking her back into a tree. I knew immediately she was hurt. She rolled over and began crying hysterically. Just then, Jocelyn, who had been pretty much silent, started throwing up everywhere. With my head buzzing with vodka, the situation seemed even more surreal, like some out-of-body experience.

I went over to Gabby to see if she was okay, but as I stooped down, she sat up quickly and slapped me in the face and gave me a bloody nose. As it dripped into my hands, the three of us heard our moms shouting for us from down the path, but we were too dizzy and sick to care too much.

It was mom's raspy voice I heard mostly. "Sheena! Sheena!" She sounded scared and angry, getting louder and louder as they came closer. And we didn't move. We were caught.

When they spotted us from the path, they came over and looked as shocked and angry as you'd expect. Mom jogged over when she saw the blood.

"What the hell happened?" She screamed.

I was never one to rat on other kids, but for some reason, I said it was Gabby.

"Sheena pushed me into the tree!" Gabby argued.

Then, as Jocelyn's mom was nursing her nauseous, vomiting child, she spotted the empty vodka bottle on the ground and picked it up and couldn't have looked more shocked and disgusted. At this point, in my inebriated state, nothing was fully registering in my mind; but for some reason, mom was now in a shoving match with Gabby's mother. Very quickly it became more than a shoving match: punches were thrown, hair was pulled, and soon the police were called, probably by a jogger or someone trying to use the nature path in peace.

After a lecture from the cops, mom dragged me to the car by the arm, leaving everything on the picnic table exactly as it was, including my pink and purple music cake.

This was the last time Gabby and Jocelyn ever spoke to me, unless you count the nasty things they'd say to me at school and after school chorus. I tried not to care, but the truth was, I really did. Chorus was no longer any fun, and it got to the point where I wanted to quit badly. I figured I'd give it until the end of the year concert before I told Mmm. But it turned out, I didn't need to.

The last night ended up happening on the night of the big concert. I knew something was wrong. By now, mom was no longer a wannabe soccer mom, and for weeks she had stopped trying even a little bit. For much of that school year, mom picked and prepped my outfits, but not that night. The night before, as mom was passed out on the couch, so on my own, I took out my favorite purple dress and white sweater. It was wrinkled, so I fired up the iron and did my best to press it and make it look nice.

Not knowing much about using an iron, I had it on the wrong setting and singed a hole somewhere around the shoulder area. Figuring the sweater would cover it up, I slipped into the dress anyhow, found my black shoes, and got ready. That morning, mom said she'd take me to the school, but in her comatose state, it seemed she needed to be reminded.

"Mom?" I whispered in her ear. "We gotta go."

"Where?" She growled, not even opening her eyes.

"My concert. It's time to leave."

She nodded but showed no sign of getting up for several minutes. I finally, shook her. "Mom! We need to leave!"

It took a while, but mom soon found the willpower to get up and throw on some sweat pants and a hoodie before getting into the car to go. The drive was terrifying. Mom, who was barely able to walk, was finding it very difficult to stay in her lane. It wasn't long before I knew that I wasn't going to make it to the concert, and I wasn't fully convinced I was going to survive the car ride.

On the dark, busy road before my school, mom seemed to have very little control of the car. Every time she'd drift too close to the center lines, I would shout at her, and she'd jerk the wheel and assure me that she didn't need my help. Then, during one of these very instances, as mom was scolding me, we heard a horn blaring and coming right at us. Mom looked up, cut the wheel, and steered the car off the road into a tree.

When I woke up in the hospital hours later, I was told that mom was 'healing' in another room and that she was okay, but I knew this wasn't true. Mom may have survived the crash, but only physically. Nothing on the inside of her was 'healing' at all—inside she was still very broken. I didn't fully understand it at the time, but some social worker in some white room told me mom wasn't able to take care of me anymore, and that she wasn't sure when she would be.

In a condescending whisper, she said I had to live and go to school somewhere different, maybe with people I didn't even know.

It was days before I gave a single thought about missing the concert.

Chapter Twenty-Six

For the next couple of weeks, I was on complete autopilot, especially at work where I could barely function. Carl, who had to be completely insane or completely desperate for help, accepted my text message apology, and I appreciated yet another chance, but not enough to give him the best version of myself—like ever. I was too tired…too tired of everything and simply going through the motions of life, existing day to day. I even began to regret ever driving to Maine in the first place and opening myself up to disappointment.

What was I thinking? At least I had some ambition before I found mom again. Now, now, I didn't care about college or my future or much of anything else. I was in too much pain to care. Thoughts of pills filled my mind more than college now, and it grew worse each day. At the bakery, whether I was making dough in the back or cashing out customers, I thought seriously about texting my connection to score Xanax.

Each time, just before this fantasy became another dumb decision, something would miraculously sidetrack me—an order from Carl, a phone call, the shop door ringing. But no matter what, my thoughts always returned to those little white tablets. I envisioned them pouring down on me like rain at a concert festival.

One day, during my cigarette break, I sat against the bakery wall behind the shop and went on to the community college website on my phone. I gazed through my exhaled smoke at campus life photos, all those anonymous kids with laptops and books, sitting against lush trees, smiling in the classroom. I wanted to be in those pictures. In many ways, I wanted to be them, to have some direction, a future.

With the fall semester just weeks away, it all seemed worse than a fantasy now, it seemed delusional. Still, whatever took my attention away from Xanax—real or not—more than justified it in my mind. That day, though, it simply wasn't enough. After work, I drove around with nothing but pills on my mind. With each mile, I could feel myself giving up, not seeing a point in resisting any longer, knowing that the guy who had always supplied me was never far.

I would like to say that I resisted, that I drove straight back to my aunt's house, ate a sandwich, and crawled into bed…but I didn't. Instead, I made the call and met my dealer who had my usual order ready to go when I pulled up to his apartment complex. Like always, he asked if I wanted to come in and play video games or watch a movie, and like always I said no thanks and headed home.

At each traffic light, at each stop sign, I would look over at the pill bottle on the passenger seat, like it was a long-lost friend, unsure if I wanted to resist or give in.

When I pulled into the driveway, I made sure my car was all the way to the left, halfway on the grass, so my aunt and uncle could pull into the garage when they came home from work. As I stepped out of the car, pills in hand, I was startled at the sight of someone relaxing in the hammock hanging between two trees on the far corner of the yard. Stopping, I looked closer and saw it was dad, napping—his long legs hanging off both sides and his Chuck Taylor's touching the grass. When I was within a couple of feet, I tried to wake him with a whisper: "Dad…"

He didn't move, so I tried again and shook the hammock gently until he lifted his head and looked at me.

He yawned. *Gabba hey*, he said, stretching his arms. *What's going on?*

"What are you doing here?" I asked.

He yawned again and said, *Thought I'd check up on you.*

"Well, things can't be any worse," I told him.

Things could always be worse…

"Not this time."

Nah, you don't know how lucky you are to be you.

I had to laugh—so I did. "Are you serious with that Dr. Phil shit?"

It's true, kid. You're an original. The real thing. A hip girl in a world of squares and drones.

I crossed my arms. "So what? None of that's done me any good."

You think those will? he said, pointing at my clenched fist that held my pills.

"What?" I said pretending to not know what he meant.

Things can get crazy fast.

I shrugged but knew he was right. "I don't know how much longer I can hold on, Dad. When you think about it, shit's out of our control. We think it's in our control, but not that much is. It's like some people are just destined for good things, some aren't. And it doesn't matter what you do about it."

Dad boosted himself up in the hammock and looked over his sunglasses at me, making this one of the few times I had seen his eyes. *You believe in all that destiny shit?* he said.

"I have no idea what I believe. I just know I'm more lost than ever."

No, you're not. I've seen lost, and you ain't lost. When you have yourself, you're good.

"I'm not sure if I do."

Think you'll find yourself in that pill bottle?

I felt caught. Ashamed. "These help me to forget about myself. And I really don't think myself is enough."

Dad moved off the hammock, took off his leather jacket, and went over to the lawn mower beside the shed. He started it up and began cutting the lawn, going back and forth until he was near me again. Stopped, with dad looking at me and the mower idling at my feet, he pointed at the pills in my hand and gestured like he wanted me to drop the bottle on the grass so he could run them over. And I nearly did. I even felt my hand move in that direction, my grip loosening.

But something—whatever you want to call that destructive impulse inside of me, that same dark impulse mom had—pulled my hand back as I clenched the pills even tighter like my life depended on them. I bolted into the house.

As much as I wanted to swallow every pill inside that bottle, I decided to wait until after I ate; it was almost like, deep down, I was still hoping for some kind of intervention, any excuse to not give in to this desire, so I went into the fridge and took out some leftover pasta. As I waited for it to heat up in the microwave, I noticed a small package on the counter; it was a thick, letter-size manila envelope, and it had my name on it.

As the microwave beeped, I stood there, stunned, realizing the scrawl on the front of it could only be mom's writing. But what was the point? Was her apology letter? A list of lame excuses? I picked it up, thinking it would be simpler to tear it up and throw it away. Then I noticed the return address was somewhere in Portland. *Why Portland?* I thought. I tore open the package which contained a sheet of lined paper, folded in thirds, and yet another sealed envelope.

I paused again, afraid to read what she had to say, afraid because whatever she had to say—whether it was 'have a nice life' or 'I love you'—it was going to be painful. Curious, I opened one corner of the other envelope, just a little and very slowly. Right away, I saw it was cash—a lot of cash, a stack of $100 bills. I flipped through them with my thumb and counted about fifty. My hand trembled when I realized I was holding thousands of dollars.

Call me crazy, but I hated the sight of that money and would have still hated it if it was $1 million. Was she really trying to pay me off? Was this like a guilt thing? Money for all the birthdays and Christmases she wasn't around for? Furious, she could think my forgiveness could be bought, I wanted to rip it all up and return it. Instead, I decided that if mom took the time to write to me, I should probably read what she had to say. But not at that moment. Not until I was ready.

Chapter Twenty-Seven

For the next couple of weeks, I kept mom's letter and her cash in a compartment inside my guitar case, right next to my pill bottle. I tried not to think about any of it, but it was useless. Regardless of how many hours I worked and how busy it got, this internal whisper kept telling me to take a few pills, *just this once.* Another voice was nagging at me to read mom's letter, but I found this idea easier to ignore. If she had something to say, why not to my face?

My aunt was also worried about me and even went so far as to sign me up for counseling.

After she begged me for an hour, I reluctantly agreed to give it a try. I guess I appreciated Aunt Laurie's effort, but I knew it would be a mistake.

Despite her black horn rim glasses and her tight pulled-back hair, the counselor didn't look much older than me. And it was just one useless question after another.

She started with, "So what's going on with you?"

"I have no idea."

"What brings you in today?"

"My aunt wanted me to."

"Do you want to be here?"

"Not really."

"Have you ever seen a counselor before?"

"At school."

"What was that like?"

"Useless."

"Overall, how would you describe your mood?"

"Sad."

"How do you know you are sad?"

"Because I feel it."

"What makes you happy?"

"I don't know."

"You don't?"

"Maybe music."

"Excellent. Anything else? If you had a magic wand, what changes would you make in your life?"

"Uh…"

I hated to be rude but I stood up and left after the magic wand question. This must've been her fastest session ever, and I'm sure she was an okay counselor, but I couldn't take it anymore. I've never been good at explaining myself, which was why I was happy Aunt Laurie wasn't there when I got home. I told her it would be a waste of money.

I went downstairs and sat on the edge of the pull-out bed, staring at my sticker-covered guitar case. Somehow, I knew I was going to open it, then open something else. After placing it flat on the floor, I flipped up the locks and opened it up, seeing my shiny acoustic there for the first time in weeks. I reached into the compartment, still unsure of myself, and after a moment of hesitation, brushed my hand past the pills and pulled out mom's letter. I guess I was ready.

My Sheena,

I'm so glad you decided to read this letter and not throw it away, even tho you'd have a right to do that. I've been wrong about almost everything in my life but I think I'm right about going away again and not telling you. Really. Please keep reading even tho this is long and you are probably mad as fuck at me. I'm a goof, I know. Just let me explain ok?

I looked up from the letter and closed my eyes. I was relieved to hear she was alive, but how much more emotional energy was I going to put into this thing? Did I have a line? I took a deep breath and tried to prepare myself for whatever she had to tell me in this barely legible letter.

I read on:

I never really told you how abusive Jim was but I bet you already knew. You're too smart to not see it. He liked to hit me a lot and I thought that he could kill me if he got mad enough. Once he locked me in the bathroom for a whole day because I pissed him off for something but I forget what because I was high. You are probably wondering why I stayed with a guy like Jim. Good question and I don't really know what to tell you.

Fear, all the drugs he gave me? both? It's not always easy to know why we do the things right? But one thing I know, he was coming for me. He was texting me saying he knows where I was and that he was coming to NH if I didn't come back.

He's crazy as fuck and would def do what he said he would do. I'd hate myself if this monster was in your life now because of me. You suffered too much already and I'm not letting that happen. I also know now and I'm sure you do that I'm powerless against the other thing I'm running from. I think about it every second and want it in me more than my own blood. Crazy huh? It's been a part of me since I was not much older than you and I don't know how to live without it.

I was hoping you or just trying to be normal would keep me from it, and it worked for a while. But to think you could keep me from something so dark is not fair. This may sound desperate but I am desperate. After days of crying myself to sleep, I decided that there are only two things that could keep me from junk...death or jail.

I dropped the letter and covered my face, afraid to read where this was going. With mom's current state of mind, anything was possible, so of course, at this point, I feared the worst. Was I really reading my mother's suicide letter? What exactly was I looking at? I just had to pause, catch my breath before I read more.

I hate to say it, but I did go back to Jim like you probably feared...but before you hate me forever, hear me out.

I actually punched the table after reading this part. I didn't want to 'hear her out"' if it had anything to do with Jim. I was tired of the bullshit and there was no excuse for her going back to that asshole, leaving me motherless, *again*. I couldn't think of a justification for sending your daughter a letter this painful. Part of me wanted to stop reading and burn the letter, but with damp, burning eyes, I kept reading anyway.

Jim picked me up a few miles down the road the day after the oven thing. I felt really shitty about that. Jim was mad at me but tried to cover it up but I knew. On the way back to Maine, he gave me some Oxy which I took and then was out. I woke up a few hours later still in the car outside the trailer, feeling like the worst piece of shit in the world. After everything I did with you, how could I just give in just like that? I felt totally unable to resist now, and if I can't resist it and feel normal even when I hate doing it so much and now have a reason to not do it (you), am I even human anymore? What am I worth?

I pictured mom in Jim's car, looking out toward her trailer, helpless and pretty much captive, unable to exercise her own free will.

Later on that night, we started fighting about something stupid and it turned into this big thing and we were screaming at each other like crazy for hours. Even when it got late, we kept fighting until I had enough and locked myself in my room. I couldn't take it anymore. I didn't want to be there but I was too scared to run out like I wanted to. It really felt like prison. My thoughts, where I lived, Jim, everything was prison.

This gave me my idea. When I knew Jim was sleeping, I went into his room and took his stupid guitar where he hides most of his supply. It felt really heavy and I knew it would be because that guys from Portland was here the earlier and he was all stocked up to move some serious shit. I dragged the thing outside and I went real slow, almost giving in, almost tearing into some of it, but I didn't.

What I did do was go into Jim's car, taking the guitar with me, locking myself inside. After lighting a cigarette, I started it up and turned on the car stereo which happened to be playing metal of course, and was already pretty damn loud. I smiled and turned it up a little, then a little more. I smiled as I saw the neighbors' lights go on in their trailers, turning it up to full volume. Within thirty seconds, Jim was outside banging on the hood, screaming at me to get the fuck out of the car.

But I didn't. I sat there and laughed, even as he tried to open the locked door with the most pissed-off face I ever saw on him. There was nothing he could do. Soon, all of my neighbors were outside in their pajamas, looking at us like we were crazy. Just when I thought he was gonna break the window with his fist, I saw Jim's eyes get big as he watched blue and red lights coming closer. The cops came sooner than I thought they would.

Scared as shit, Jim turned and ran inside to hide the shit that was all out in the open, stuff that could get him some crazy jail time. I felt like I was inside an episode of COPS. Then, as the cruiser pulled in, I jumped out holding Jim's heroin-filled acoustic like an ax. I felt so crazy, like I was onstage again with my heart about to pound out of my chest.

And just as the officer opened his door, I smashed the guitar like I used to on the rear bumper of Jim's car, making the bags of powder fly everywhere, including at the cops feet as he came closer. He saw piles of heroin all over the dirt and knew exactly what he was looking at. I don't think he ever saw so much heroin in one place.

I looked up from the letter again, immediately recalling the video at the record store of mom destroying that guitar. All the angst she had back then, all the juice of life that had disappeared, I imagined it returning to her as she fucked up Jim's acoustic, and I imagined her screaming in the process, going completely primal as the cops and neighbors watched in awe. I read on:

In less than five minutes, his backup was there and me and Jim were arrested. Besides the mother-load I smashed out on the car, they found pills, crack, and even an unregistered gun in Jim's bags and stuff. I knew we'd be in a whole lot of deep shit, but I knew Jim would be in deeper shit. We were brought to the police station and I was charged with drug possession. Jim was charged with a lot more and was denied bail. I didn't want bail, so I was locked up in county waiting for my arraignment.

You probably think I'm crazy for doing something like this on purpose but I was desperate. I'd do anything to keep that shit away from me, and hopefully, I won't want it after some time in here. If you're pissed at me, I get it. You have every right to be. I hope it will fade over time and that you can forgive me if I get better. I promise I will try like hell to be better for you. I hope you use that cash. It's all for you to go to school with.

Please use it to help you be what you want to be; something not like me. Soon I swear, I will come back to you when I'm out of here and I'm sober enough to be your mom. I don't want to be a junky anymore. I want to be your mom.

I love you, Mom

In shock, I folded the letter and placed it next to me on the bed. Leave it to mom to do something this extreme. Predicting her was impossible, but this was another level of crazy, even for her. Apparently, rehab was too conventional for her so she went and had herself arrested by pulling a Pete Townsend on a car. Part of me thought it would be easier to get rid of the money, to donate it or something. Did I really want all this?

A relationship with her was always going to be one thing after another. What if she spent two years in jail and was still a junky when she got out? What if I was still kind of a junky, too? Why should I put up with it? How much faith do you put in a person? I was confused as ever, but I still, by some miracle, resisted the urge to take the pills I had just scored.

Chapter Twenty-Eight

I lost myself in my routine for much of August. Mom's letter and the cash were tucked away in my guitar case, and not once did I open the letter or take out my guitar. I was too uninspired to face either of those things. Still, I couldn't put mom out of my head; I wondered how long she'd be in jail for, unsure if it was a matter of months or years. My aunt went to visit her twice at the prison in Portland, and both times I refused to go, and I wasn't sure why.

Maybe it was because I didn't want to see mom in an orange jumpsuit or somehow explain why I did not deposit her cash—not that I knew why. With so much to say to each other, I wasn't sure I wanted to talk on a prison phone from behind the glass.

Then it struck me. Something hit me hard at the end of a long shift at the bakery as I was sliding a tray of dough onto a rack.

I'm avoiding. Again. Like usual, I just don't want to face what's hard. This is what mom used to do, but she changed...I think. Have I?

I decided then I wasn't going to wait for my aunt to visit Mom again. I would go myself.

After my shift, I went home and took a picture of the address written on my aunt's little refrigerator whiteboard. I then looked up the prison visiting hours on my phone and took the next day off from work. After a two-hour ride the next day, I pulled into the prison entrance and was stopped at a checkpoint by some grumpy guard who looked like a mastiff, who then directed me toward a small lot near the visitor's entrance.

It was there I took a deep breath before going in, emptying my pockets, and going through a metal detector. I was then led into a sterile waiting area where I sat staring out the window for more than thirty minutes.

Soon, I looked up and saw her. Even though I tried to prepare myself, it was no use at all. Seeing my mother on the other side of that glass wall, dressed like some convict, was completely surreal and painful. It was still nice to see her smiling at me as each step she took was controlled by the guard who led her over and onto the chair like she was a child. He gestured at me to go over, so I did with mom's eyes following me as I sat down.

Through the glass, she looked much healthier—even had a slight glow and wasn't as gaunt. She picked up the receiver and pointed at the wall phone on my side of the glass.

There was an awkward silence, both of us waiting for the other to speak first, like we were trying to read each other's mind, like we were in a staring contest. Finally, it was mom who spoke up:

"I know what you're thinking. What the fuck, right?" She said, almost laughing about it. I didn't see the humor.

"Yeah, what the fuck pretty much sums it up," I said.

She nodded in agreement. "I'm kinda at a loss here."

"*You're* at a loss?" I said.

"It's tough, trying to explain why anyone would go to jail…like on purpose," she said.

"Maybe I am crazy." She put her hands over her face and started laughing.

Not seeing the humor, I asked: "It had to be like this? This is supposed to be a solution?"

Mom's smile disappeared as she thought about my question deeply. "I don't know," she said. "Maybe. Maybe not. But I am so happy you're here. I missed you."

My eyes started watering when she said that. It was nice to be missed. It was nice to feel loved, even from the other side of the prison glass.

Noticing my tears, she said, "I'm sober, kiddo, like for real now."

I looked up but stopped myself from becoming too excited. Of course, she was sober; she had no choice. But does it count? Would it even last?

"Good…" I said, wiping my eyes.

"The hell it's been, Sheena, I can't even describe it," she said. "But you really do start to feel stuff again. The numbness wears off and the emptiness too, slowly. I have these bad moments every day, mostly at night, but I have good moments too. That's almost normal, right? I almost feel real again."

"What next then?" I asked.

Mom looked up at the ceiling like she had to think about it. "Sentencing is next week, but I'll get a chunk of time. Prior convictions and all that."

"After that?"

She smiled. "I'm coming back—to you. For real, kiddo. I wanna be your mother, like a real mother…or something like one. I wanna go places with you. Play music. See your report card."

I shot her a *yeah right* look.

"Did you sign up for classes?" She asked.

I shook my head. "I'm not gonna get a report card," I said rubbing my forehead. "You can have all that money back." After a while, you start to feel like an idiot believing people. But something inside me did believe her, at least a little. My smile faded as my eyes drifted down her arms as she rolled up her orange sleeves. Her scars, where the needles tore, had faded; they were not ruby red but a faint pink.

They were there to be sure, but they were old scars now, nearly blended into her pale skin. Noticing I was looking there, she floated her fingers over these wounds, not ashamedly—but lovingly, proudly. Not once did she claw at herself, like so many times before.

"It's what you wanted, Sheena," she said. "Right?"

"I guess," I said.

"Do you believe me?" She asked moving closer to the window, "when I say I'm coming back to you?"

Sitting there, it felt like I had a choice to make. I could go on thinking that mom was nothing more than a junky and would always be a junky, that dysfunction was her default setting and it would always amount to her leaving me. Or I could believe her.

I nodded.

Mom smiled and looked relieved. "Will you promise your mother something?"

I stared down at the floor. "What?"

She hesitated like it was something very serious. "As soon as you leave here, go right to that college. Sign up for whatever the hell it is you want to do. What will be your major anyway?"

I looked down at my feet. "Music."

"Please do it. Listen to your mother."

After giving me a stern look, she smiled and pressed her hand against the glass. After a moment of hesitation, I put my hand over hers and pressed hard.

Chapter Twenty-Nine

If you're not me—a girl who's never lived on a cul-de-sac and who doesn't know any Tik-Tok dances—it might be hard to understand why I didn't go straight to the bank to deposit my mom's cash and then immediately enroll at the college like she told me to. Wasn't this what I wanted all along? Shouldn't I have jumped at the chance? But the truth is, I didn't even go the next day or the day after that.

Instead, I went to work at the bakery, then I went home. I ate leftovers. Went to bed early. I did what I always did. Nothing special. If you're not me, it may be impossible to get why I hesitated, unsure if I really wanted to commit to something so new, something real. Was I worried it would also be a commitment to mom? If I was to take her up on this, was I ready to take on all this in the long-term, all the good and all the bad?

When I came home late one afternoon, my aunt was in the living room, sitting on the couch doing nothing except—so it seemed—waiting for me. Her concerned expression stopped me in my tracks as the screen door closed behind me.

"What?" I asked bluntly. If there was more bad news, I wanted her to just say it.

"We should bring grandma somewhere," she said.

"What are you talking about?" I asked.

My aunt gestured toward the urn on the mantle. "It's silly to keep her up there in a container doing nothing."

I wasn't catching on. "What else should she be doing?"

She seemed a bit hesitant to tell me. "I think we should, you know…"

"Spread her ashes?" I said, catching on, trying to help her.

"Yes, exactly," she said.

"Where?" I asked.

She got up, took grandma off the mantle, and clung to her with both hands. "I think I know. But will you come with me, please? I don't want to do it alone. It wouldn't feel right."

I understood this, but mom immediately came to mind. "Don't you think you should wait for my mom to get out of jail, whenever that'll be? Shouldn't she be a part of this?"

"She doesn't want to go."

"And you asked her?"

"Of course, Sheena. I wouldn't do this without her involvement."

"And she doesn't want to be…involved?"

"She said it's not her thing, but she did feel strongly about where."

"Ok, then where?"

She sat back down with the urn on her lap. "We don't have many great memories as a family, so there's no magical place that jumped out at me. But your mother reminded me of the time we went to Lakeside Park one day when it was still open, way before you were born." I knew exactly the place she meant.

Although, it had been long shuttered up, much of it was still there, derelict, a ghost of an amusement park. And like most kids in town, I would sneak in all the time, ignoring the *No Trespassing* sign, just so I could roam underneath what was left of the old wooden roller coaster.

"You want to dump her ashes *there*?" I asked.

"I don't want to think of it as dumping. But it may be one of the only places I remember seeing her happy—or should I say *us* happy. It seems to make sense, I guess, to spread her remains there. It's as good a place as any, right?"

I guess this made some sense. The next day, with grandma now on *my* lap, Aunt Laurie drove us across town toward the lake and up to the chained up gates of what was left of Lakeside Park. We parked and then hiked past the old graffiti-covered sign, stepping over broken beer bottles and used condoms. After a few minutes of following my aunt—who didn't seem to have a very specific idea of where we were going to do this—we stopped at a picnic table next to the shell of a horseless carousel.

I placed grandma on the table as we looked around, finding it hard to imagine that the place was once filled with laughter and music.

"We went on this thing a lot, your mother and me…over and over again," she said. "Maybe it's my imagination but I remember seeing your grandmother smiling at us as we went around."

My aunt picked up the urn and took off the cover. "I guess we better do this before the cops bust us," she said.

"Right here?" I asked.

She nodded, gave herself some space and flung the ashes everywhere in a circular direction. A slight breeze came and wafted some of grandma into a nearby patch of overgrown grass and weeds as the rest of her fell into the soot and shallow puddles upon the old concrete.

With the urn still in her hand, my aunt hugged me. She hugged me like we've been close all along. It felt kind of weird, but I guess I was okay with that.

I suppose you'll hug anyone when you need one bad enough, when you're clinging to one nice memory, one smile, when that's all you have from someone who should've given you more. And I suppose this was one reason why I went home immediately after my shift at the bakery and dumped my pills into the toilet.

The next morning, I pulled into the community college parking lot, turned off the car and sat there still and scared. As of 9:07 am, my checking account had far more money in it than ever before, but for some reason, I still felt hesitant, unsure of myself and pretty much everything. The campus looked so big and I didn't see one familiar face among the students striding in and out of the buildings.

It wasn't a panic attack, but I was getting there, so I did my deep breathing. And just as I was calming myself down, a car pulled up beside me to my left, an unbelievably loud car. When I looked over, I saw that it was dad, behind the wheel of some old 50's convertible, like the kind you see in *Grease*.

Hey, kiddo! He had to shout over the car's roaring engine.

"Dad?"

Don't let them change you too much in there, he said with a smirk.

"Who says I'm going in?" I asked.

He peeked over his sunglasses at me and said, *Listen to your mother*.

As he peeled out and drove off, after the exhaust cleared, I noticed his car had a New York license plate. I figured that's where he went that day because I've never seen him since.

After a few minutes of deliberating, I decided to listen to my mother. More importantly, I decided to listen to myself. I figured it must be okay to live with uncertainty—without knowing if everything was going to work out. Like a rock star with a healthy amount of stage fright, I marched inside the school and signed up for classes with every reason to believe that mom would soon be around for as long as I needed her.